Slippery When Wet

a Brazen Boys story

by Daryl Banner

Books By Daryl Banner

Slippery When Wet: a Brazen Boys story

This book is a work of fiction.
Names, characters, groups, businesses, and incidents
either are the product of the author's imagination or are
used fictitiously. Any resemblance to actual places or
persons, living or dead, is entirely coincidental.

Cover & Interior Design : Daryl Banner

Cover Model : Nick Duffy
www.instagram.com/nickduffyfitness

Photo of Nick Duffy by Simon Barnes

Slippery When Wet

a Brazen Boys story

by Daryl Banner

[Sand]

I would reach for his face, but the ropes are too tight.

"Let go of all control," he tells me. "Only when you've let go of everything, can you keep hold of anything."

I'm tied to the bed, naked as my birthday. I'm terrified and I'm excited and my cock is harder than it's ever been, and this dude wants to fucking philosophize.

His warm lips brush my neck, right by my tingling ears, and in that deep voice of his, he says: "You're mine."

All my life, I've been the sand: dry and unforgiving when caught in the eyes. But I desperately want to be the ocean. There is so much freedom in the reckless crashing of waves, a freedom I don't understand. There is a beauty in the chaos that terrifies a control freak like me. I would never let a guy tie me up in real life no matter how gorgeous he is, no matter how kind.

It's fear and it's reason that keep me from offering use of both my hands to a beautiful stranger. It's fear and it's reason that keep the most of us alive and safe.

Safe as sand on a beach.

"Let go," he breathes into my ear, then straddles my naked chest, a thick and powerful thigh on either side. "I'm taking over, now." Where most fantasy college guys wear a six-pack of beer, this one's got one of a different sort playing up his front. He's perfect. He's ... *too* perfect.

That's because this is a dream. And I'm controlling it one hot desire at a time.

"I'm going to give you a night you'll never forget," he tells me, and he grins devilishly because I want him to. "And there's nothing you can do about it."

But there is something I can do about it. Something quite easy, in fact. I can wake up.

"You're all mine."

I can wake up, and the use of my hands will be instantly returned to me. Even when someone else is totally in control, I am still in control.

His lips crash into mine. My heart flutters and my wrists pull against the ropes. I feel the deep and penetratingly artificial sensation of helplessness. I moan against his mouth. His wicked hands run down the length of my torso. It tickles slightly because I let it. His hands reach my thighs. They go everywhere but my cock because I love the tease, I crave the foreplay, I go crazy for the chase. *Keep chasing me, dream boy. Don't let me off so easy.*

"You ready?" he breathes into my face, and his breath is perfect. I hate when you're all into someone and then they breathe on you and you're introduced to the seventh gate of hell for a second.

I'll never be ready. There is electricity in his fingertips, and everywhere he dares to touch, I respond with a gasp and a moan and a plea that never leaves my lips. I pull on my wrists and ankles deliberately to remind myself of the sexy, helpless predicament in which I've put myself.

For twenty-one years I've not been ready. My twenty-second birthday is a couple days away and I'm still not ready. Gripping onto every armrest, clinging onto every keystroke when I type my school papers, gluing my eyes to every sexy boy my age that I'll never let myself speak to ... this is the soil in which I've planted these dream boys of mine, these dream boys who do whatever I want ... *in my head.*

These dreams are my love life, because a real love life is too full of messiness, accidents, pain, and embarrassment. I get easily annoyed. I'm critical. It feels so inorganic and ugly as an ancient armoire you're trying to get rid of in a garage sale, but no one nabs it no matter how low you mark the price tag slapped onto it.

"You ready? Come on, buddy," he says, and his hand comes dangerously close to my cock, barely grazing my tight balls, sending shivers of anticipation up my body. "Let go. All you gotta do is let go, and then you can—"

The alarm clock goes off.

My eyes shoot open.

[Mannequin]

I'm officially on vacation in three hours with my best friend Ollie, and that alarm clock I set last night is reminding me so.

And *loudly*. Damn.

I put on the clothes I set out for myself the night before. (I had my outfit planned for a week, in fact.) I check my luggage after eating breakfast, as if ensuring my underwear hadn't magically returned to the dresser. Not that going commando for seven days on a ship in the middle of the gulf is the worst thing. My breakfast consists of one hard-boiled egg and a precise amount of orange juice I portioned out so as not to leave any remaining in the fridge while I'm gone. I switch off every appliance but the fridge, unplug every cord from the wall, and double check every power strip.

Then I do it all again, just to be sure.

The ship is enormous. Summer's almost over. The sun is bright. This'll be the perfect vacation ever. This is what I recite to myself seven lucky times before leaving the house behind ... and my dreams, which still writhe somewhere in the bed I made after my abrupt awakening. "*Let go,*" the dream boy seems to whisper in my ears, but while I am awake, the world looks so, so different. *I can't let go, dumb dream. So much depends on me, don't you understand? I'll always be the dry sand. You'll always be the sea.*

Standing at the door, I go over the lists in my head, just to be triple sure. It's like that moment before you leave and you're thinking: *I know I'm forgetting something. I just know it.*

In the car on the three-plus hour trip to Galveston, I call Ollie six times, and six times the flakey tech-geek fart-bag doesn't answer. *I have my passport. He better have his. And the boarding passes, too.* It was a mistake to let him handle all the business, but it's *his* employer that offered the discount, and I'm trying this new thing called "trust".

After high school, he offered me a space in the big roomy house his parents left him in Houston, but being the stubborn dick that I am, I insisted on moving away to Austin. It's times like this that make me question my decision, since I would be there ensuring he didn't forget anything. Then, we'd be driving together ... if I trusted his taste in road music.

I stretch a big dumb smile across my rigid face to coax myself into a better mood. I take a deep breath and I let it all out on the steering wheel, which I grip tight as a strangler's intent. *We're going to have the perfect vacation. Nothing is going to fuck it all up.*

Something fucks it all up. I find Ollie waiting in front of the cruise ship terminal. He wears an orange tank that makes his dark skin shine. A flashy bathing suit hangs to his knees. Yellow flip-flops decorate his feet and his hair is nonexistent—buzzed to the scalp. His only luggage is a backpack on his shoulder and a light smile. Other than the rare Skype chat, Ollie and I have seen little of each other in the past year, since he stayed in Houston for college and I insisted on going to Austin.

I hardly notice the lady-person at his side.

"Oh!" Even before saying hello to Ollie, I pay mind to the presence of his girlfriend since high school. Twenty-two years young, she's six feet of beige plastic with needle-thin arms, a curly up-do, and enormous black sunglasses that scream "rich bitch". Trish is her name. I call her The Mannequin. "You've come to see us off! How sweet of you."

"No, man." Ollie's voice is still squeaky as the day we met in an elementary school classroom, though maybe an octave lower now that years have happened. "Cabin's for three."

I don't follow, staring at him blankly until my eyes finally drift to the fat set of cheetah print luggage squatting by The Mannequin's chalky chicken legs.

Trish twists her neck. "Ollie. You didn't tell him? Seriously?"

"He doesn't mind," my friend insists. "The more, the merrier. Am I right?" Ollie slaps a hand on my shoulder, knocking me out of my cheetah print trance. "Am I right?"

It was supposed to be just us guys. Buddies sharing the adventure of a cruise for the first time. Laughing at drunken fools on the lido deck. Him, checking out the gals because Trish won't know. Me, checking out the bros because ... bros. Sharing midnight pizza on the deck with the cool gulf wind on our faces.

The fantasy didn't include Malibu Barbie.

Let go, whispers the dream voice from deep within. "You're right!" I insist. Trish and I have had enough squabbles and dirty *bitch-please* looks for a lifetime. Maybe we can set aside our childish enmity for seven tiny days and just have fun. "More the merrier."

"He's pissed," says Trish with a sneer.

"No, no," I say, not quite trusting myself to meet her eyes so soon—or, in this case, her giant *can't-be-bothered* sunglasses that make her look like a wasp that's stung every hairdresser from here to Los Angeles. "Ollie's right. Let's get ourselves through the embarkation process, alright? The sooner we do, the sooner we'll have mojitos in our hands!"

She smirks. "I'm allergic to mint."

I can't even. "The beverage of your choice then," I amend with a tight smile. "Let's go! Not gonna let a little bump ruin our day."

"I'm a little bump?"

We're going to have the perfect vacation. I ignore her and lead the way, my luggage rolling noisily on the pavement behind me, the left wheel dragging lazily the wrong way. *Breathe in, breathe out.* The big dumb smile happens on my face again after we get through the passport line. I grip my luggage handle so tight, my wrist cramps painfully.

Then I see him.

"No, you all go ahead. We'll take the next

one," says Ollie to the bunch of dude-bros ahead of us getting on the elevator. Among the dude-bros, there is a guy who stings my eyes and stabs me in the heart just by existing. It's as if the boy who tied me to a bed in my dreams has somehow physicalized—a god who's taken human form for this one instant as he enters the elevator with his friends. His back turned, he doesn't see me, listening to a joke his buddy tells him. He breaks into a fit of cute guffawing as the doors slide shut.

My underarms turn into lakes. Steam magically fills my shorts. Heat hits my cheeks and threatens to drench my hair in sweat.

I could've crammed in there with those boys. I so would have welcomed it. I would have positioned myself in just the right way so that I would be helplessly sandwiched against that hot slab of boy-beef.

Eight and a half precious minutes later, I am very happy to report that I rediscover him ahead of us in the pre-boarding line. Watching him puts me in such a deep state of bro-consciousness, I don't pay mind to Ollie's rambling, nor to Trish's periodic interjecting and griping. My eyes glued to the specimen of hunk ahead of me, I imagine a hundred scenarios on the ship where the two of us might meet and engage in R-rated ... things.

Perhaps involving beds and rope.

Note to self: *add that idea to the spank bank.*

I'm caught in a mind-incapacitating trance that mysteriously mutes the blathering of my best friend. Doesn't matter, I don't care what brand of dog food Ollie got for the pet sitter or how much he'll miss his little puppy for the next seven days while we're floating in the gulf. My attention is much too trapped by the guy three groups ahead of us in line.

I seriously can't look away. Maybe it's the totally skimpy white tank he wears. It's one of those tanks that's more like a sleeveless shirt with armholes that hang nearly to the hips, scant, unsubtle, loose, giving more than just a tease of his ribs and slender hips and tight pecs and popping nipples every time he moves. A pair of white sunglasses rests atop his tousled head of dirty blond hair which, while buzzed high around the sides and back, looks messy and overdue for a cut in the front, which I can't quite see as he's turned away chatting with the dude-bros he came with.

I wonder if this is all my life will ever be: a series of hot guys I study from a distance and add to my dream world where I can control everything that happens, from the meeting them to the courting them to the sexing them. In real life, I only stare and hope, hopelessly. The moment we board the cruise ship, I'll never see him again, this hot guy with the glasses and the killer arms and the messy hair.

Or, even worse, I'll see him a hundred times. I'll see him having fun with his buddies, desperately wishing I were one of them. He'll meet a girl—which inevitably happens to guys who look like him—and then I'll suffer from a distance and imagine what he tastes like.

In fact, I'll have seven exciting nights to decide precisely what he will taste like, while doing things to myself in the shower.

After the hot guy finishes the checking-in process with his buds, he disappears from my life while I stare after him longingly—until Ollie yanks on my sleeve because we've been called up next to show our boarding passes.

New relationship status: it's complicated, with ... my dreams.

[The Chase
& The Sea]

An hour and twenty minutes later, we're already within the lobby of the ship. I won't blame the presence of a whining plastic girl in our midst for my having missed the splendor of gawping at the size of the ship as we passed from the hall to the bridge-thing to the deck. I certainly won't blame Ollie and his unabashed self-centeredness on my having missed some greeting or warning or something from a hot Ukrainian fellow in a vest at the entrance.

"You alright, buddy?"

I'm so trapped in my own head that I barely hear Ollie's question. "Yes," I answer vaguely, dragging my luggage behind me through the mess of people in the lobby, which has a circle of balconies overhead that extend up ten floors. Four glass elevators lined with glowing lights and gaudy gold trimming run up the throat of the ship. I studied the map online and memorized the whole layout of the ship, having preplanned our first three days. There's so many things to do and such a high chance to miss out on fun activities, I felt it crucial to make a plan of the most efficient use of our time.

While staring upwards in a daze, I almost trip over the foot of some man in a chair who clutches his wife's purse to his chest and scowls at everything. On one end of the lobby is a crescent-shaped bar with two frantic suit-and-bowtied bartenders hastily getting many arrangements of colored alcohols into hands.

"Want to grab some drinks, man?"

I'm still smiling tight. I'm so determined to enjoy all of this. "We still got our luggage," I point out, trying to take in the sights around me. So much noise. So much chatter. So many bright and shining things to marvel at. The pictures online were one thing, but the reality is something else. The lobby is like a shopping mall, except crammed into the belly of a ship. For some reason, I was expecting the inside to look more like ... well, like a ship.

"I don't think our rooms are gonna be ready until one o'clock," Ollie says back. "Isn't that what the thingy said?"

We come to a stop. Swarms of kids and cackling women and snorting men surround us like hounds. I wonder if the hot guy and his buddies are here or have gone up to the lido already. "Isn't that just a half hour from now?"

"I want a water with lemon," volunteers Trish, unasked.

"I know, sweetie." Ollie gives Trish a peck on the lips. She flinches, which I suppose is her way of returning it. "And you, Scott?"

Scott's me. I'm Scott. Hi. "I don't care what it is," I answer. "Something with an umbrella in it."

I'm trying to "let go" and trust Ollie with the choice of beverage. Also, I may or may not still be looking for the hot guy from the line.

"Coming right up." Ollie disappears into the crowd toward the bar, he and his little backpack that somehow carries all the clothes he'll need for seven days. That punk better not be asking for my underwear by Wednesday.

The drinks take so long to get to our hands that by the time they do, we're ready to make way to our room. When we finally reach the door, I've taken exactly two sips from my fruity mystery concoction sans umbrella because, while adjusting the strap on his backpack, Ollie's hand thwacked my glass and the cute ornament flung to the floor. Despite my annoyance, I laughed it off and said it's a good thing it isn't raining or else my drink would get wet. Ollie snorted and Trish was not amused—or else didn't get the joke.

Once inside the room, I'm a bit stunned at the miscalculation I've made of exactly how narrow the cabin would be. I note the two skinny beds and a plastic couch, upon which Trish has already slapped her cheetah print bag-on-wheels. *I'll have to reimagine my nightly slumber situation for the next seven days.* We splurged and got a balcony room, thanks to Ollie's company discount. Sunlight pours in through the window and glass door, dressing the tiny slit of a cabin in yolk yellow.

"What a view!" exclaims Ollie, bringing himself to the bed by the window where he dumps his backpack, staking his claim, I guess. He sets his drink on the counter—which is a water with lemon, by the way, to match his girlfriend's exciting beverage of choice. *"We're on a cleanse,"* he had told me in the lobby when I realized I was the only one holding a glass containing anything with a taste. *"Bad week to go on a cleanse, you think?"* His nervous laugh suggested it was Trish's idea and not his.

What. The. Fuck. Ever.

I slurp on my drink—my third slurp since I was handed it, to be exact—then set it on the narrow counter by a pamphlet of things-to-do provided by the cruise line. The drink tastes terrible, though I'm not really a good judge as I hardly ever drink. I knew I should've picked my own; I can't trust Ollie to make a choice to save my life. I grab the pamphlet up and start thumbing through it, curious.

"The beds are tiny," complains Trish.

"Yeah, I know." Ollie rummages through his backpack for something. "But we can take the one by the window, sweetie, and—"

"That bed isn't going to fit both of us."

I poke a finger at the pamphlet. "Hey. They have a *Welcome Aboard!* show in the theater at the aft end of the ship. Is that the front or the back?"

Ollie has a different concern. "Uh, do you mind taking the couch, dude?"

I note the tragic couch-thing sandwiched between the closest bed and the wall in all its plastic, cadmium-yellow glory, and swallow hard. My grip on the pamphlet tenses, causing it to crinkle in protest. I hate these questions where there's really only one answer.

"I … don't mind at all," I lie.

"He's pissed," mutters Trish, her mantra of the day.

I ignore her and force myself to assume a kind expression. "You two can push the beds together. Or we can ask the stewards to do it, if we're not allowed to. I think the couch is meant to house the third person, anyway. Just needs to be … converted to a bed. We'll ask the steward. Done! No problem!"

I smile at them both, determined for today to be amazing. I still have that hot guy to stalk. Maybe he's on the lido deck right now with his buddies, drinking in the sun.

"Y'know what, guys?" I go on. "I think we're overdue for some lunch on the lido. That sounds just *great*. I'm starved, aren't you? Then, we'll go to our assigned muster station where they have that mandatory meeting about what to do in case of an emergency.

That should end in time for us to watch the ship set sail, so we'll be on the lido for a while, which should then bring us to dinner time, six or so if I had to reckon. We can do dinner in the dining room tonight and save the lido deck buffet for tomorrow, perhaps? After dinner, we'll be just in time to catch the *Welcome Aboard!* show at seven. How's that sound?"

The two of them stare blankly. I'm used to the look. It's the *quit-scheduling-every-minute-of-our-lives* look. Ollie's given it to me since we were kids, and that's saying something. None of his friends could figure out why he still hangs with me: Scott, the uptight kid who never went out after ten at night, who plans his outfits the day before, whose heart is dry as sand and hasn't had a date since sophomore year of high school. That date was beyond humiliating, by the way. I dressed up in a suit and tie and met the dude at a movie theater. His name was Kale. I spilled buttered popcorn all over myself. The stained tie still hangs in my closet. I let it remind me of that day.

It's not for lack of feelings and desire. I feel a lot. I desire a lot. I see hot guys on campus all day long, but I can never muster the courage to speak to a single one. I always wait for them to come to me, hoping some magical quality I have catches their eye.

I'm a baited hook floating lazily in an ocean full of people who've learned to swim.

But that's okay. I've gotten along for many years without the distraction of love. Really, how the hell do people do it? Boyfriends are so time-consuming. You can't make grades like I do and also have a guy waiting at home when you want to study. They're so needy, too.

Ask me the atomic number of anything on the Periodic Table and I'll spit it back at you like a fireball. I might even give you the atomic mass. Cadmium. Vanadium. Xenon. I know all about the elements.

And for a boy who knows his chemistry to know absolutely nothing about *chemistry*, well, therein lies the great and comical irony of Scott. Scott's hilarious.

By the time we've put lido buffet food into our bellies, it's already time to report to our muster stations. Yes, not two hours after getting on the boat, we're then taught how to get the fuck off—in the unlikely event of fire, sinking, or sea monster.

No, I haven't seen the hot guy again. Not on the lido deck. Not at the muster station, even though there's several of them. All I know for a fact is, he's somewhere on this ship with a gaggle full of dude-bros, and they're having a lot of fun that I'm not having.

Let's be honest. There are thousands of people on this ship, and among them, I'm bound to discover at *least* four or five other guys that could steal my undies. Even in my own muster station, there was a guy with freckles and bright, enormous eyes who robbed all my attention. I likely missed some crucial detail about how to wear the lifejackets. I'll thank him and his freckles later when I'm, y'know, drowning. On the lido deck during lunch, I spotted a meathead who works out approximately twenty-two times a day—that might be a gross underestimation—and he walked by our table in a tank top that's sure to be suffering every second of its stretched-to-the-max life. His feet carried a juggernaut's weight. The whole ship tips in his favor.

We find a nice spot at the outer railing of the panorama, which is a ring of upper deck that overlooks the lido. As we feel the engine roar and the world begin to float, we cheer and wave goodbye to the Galveston docks. Even Trish waves excitedly as the ship pushes away from shore, a sort of life returning to her eyes that had been missing since our cold meeting at the terminal. *Let's keep her like this for seven days and we might have a decent time, yet.* Ollie tells a joke to me and we both laugh, even though I missed what he said.

Then he leans in. "Hey, remember that time when we got away from our parents and climbed up that old clock tower and the world looked so fucking far away?"

We were eight. "Yeah?"

"This is, like, at *least* ten times better than that."

A thumping surge of yesteryear's club remixes fills the lido deck below, and soon a crowd of drunken fools are doing line dances in front of the pool. Ollie and I relocate to get a better view of the lido, Trish mercifully opting to stay at the outer rail. We make fun of the people dancing, sharing laughs and cackling into the noise of people cheering and laughing, unheard. *This is how I wanted it*, I realize. *Just me and Ollie. This is what our whole vacation was supposed to be like. I miss him.*

I struggle to get my head around Trish's existence, thoughtfully considering what I could do to make things easier, to help Trish stay in a good mood, to keep from throwing myself overboard. I gotta plan my course of action. I must calculate it. We are just the chemicals bouncing around in our minds, bullying our emotions and muscles and nerves. There is some secret thing I can do to make our time here ideal; I just need to figure it out.

"That guy looks like your type," says Ollie with a chortle.

I try to follow his line of sight. "Who?"

Then, I see him. The hot guy from the line. Amidst the crowd of dancers we were just making fun of, the hot guy in the skimpy sleeveless tank and the bright white sunglasses dances. I don't know what the current dance is, but it has to do with wobbling, and I'm instantly dropped-of-jaw at the sight of him.

His hips move with the finesse of sex. His legs, meaty and taut in those shorts of his, bend with the music, feet firmly planted. His arms roll in the air to the left, then to the right. He grins the whole time, his face reddened by the sun, his cute button nose pinching and wrinkling up adorably every time he laughs.

"He's alright," I say, utterly transfixed.

"You're just playing it cool," teases Ollie, knowing me too well to let my nonchalance slide. "He's giving you a total bone-bone right now, isn't he."

"Leave me and my bone-bone alone-lone."

"Hey. I know you and Trish don't—"

"It's okay," I say too quickly. I really don't prefer to spend seven days convincing him that everything's okay when it's not.

"I should've told you. I thought I did, to be honest. You know how forgetful I am, dude. I was looking forward to this cruise so much, since neither of us have taken one, and—well, honestly, I thought you would have assumed that she was coming, since—"

Ollie and I have probably talked over a hundred times about how fun this trip would be. Not *once* did he mention his girlfriend. But I keep the words to myself, not wanting to pick a fight and further antagonize the already insufferable Mannequin and my best friend.

"Know what I mean?" Ollie finishes.

I wasn't listening. I don't know what he means. "Of course." I smile vaguely, keeping my eyes glued to the spectacle on the dance floor. The hot guy moves his hips, rolls his arms in the air, laughs adorably, his face scrunching up and his tongue hanging out. Where are all his buddies?

"Totally your type," says Ollie.

I look at Ollie. He's stifling a laugh, as if proud he's caught me staring. "It'll be time for dinner soon," I point out, changing the subject entirely. "Want to head back to the room and change? I heard the line for the dining room can get pretty long unless you get there early. I read a review about this man from Illinois—"

"Actually, Trish is worried she might feel some seasickness," says Ollie, "and doesn't want to risk whatever the dining room's serving. Something about non-organic meats. I'm not sure, bud. I think we might head back to the cabin, grab a little salad later, maybe around seven or eight, if that's cool?"

It's so not cool. None of it is cool. "But ... But what about the show?" I argue back, miffed. "We were going to watch the—"

"I think it repeats at nine. We looked at the pamphlet thingy. We could watch the second performance at nine, maybe?"

Once again, I'm feeling trapped. Asked questions that have only one answer. My jaw tightens and my nerves tingle with annoyance. There's a reason we plan. Plans are necessary. Without one, we'd have missed boarding the ship. If the nine o'clock show is filled up and there's no seating, we will miss the show completely. Plans are under our noses every minute of our lives. It's the reason internet works. It's the reason phones operate. Careful planning and focus and calculations are how buildings stand up, roofs protect us from rain, and ships stay fucking afloat.

Without planning, we'd be extinct.

"I can tell that you're pissed," says Ollie quietly, "and I don't mean to—"

"Who are you? Trish? I'm not pissed. I just wish things could go the way I expected for once." I fold my arms and lean against the rail, the thumping of music sending tremors up my elbows.

"How about we relax and do our own things tonight," suggests Ollie, "and, like, when we're settled in and feeling more chill tomorrow, we can have a day of doing stuff on our ... uh, itinerary. Is that cool?"

My eyes find the hot guy on the dance floor again, and suddenly ... very suddenly ... everything is cool. *Let go.* I think about all the fun fantasies I can come up with in the shower later when I'm thinking of my dream boys, of rope and beds, of whispers in the ear and the flushing of my face. All at once, everything is brilliantly, perfectly, wonderfully, diabolically, sexily cool.

"Yes," I agree, letting a smile happen on my face, except perhaps this one is more genuine. "Sounds great, actually."

"Y'know. You could go down there and dance, too." Ollie says this in my ear. "Maybe he has a name."

"Hell-a no." I laugh. "I have two left feet and the musicality of a cricket."

"Hey now, crickets sing every night." He nudges me with an elbow. "Get a drink or two in you, maybe you'll change your mind."

Ollie leaves me with that, joining Trish at the other rail for a while before finally leaving to go who-knows-where. After the wobbling song ends, the crowd disperses and, in a panic, I lose sight of the hot guy. Dread fills me as my eyes comb through the crowd of heads from above, searching for him. What am I without my object of obsession?

Feeling my current locale to be inadequate suddenly, I stroll down the stairs to the lido, daring myself into the crowds of shirtless, wet people wrapped in towels and bathing suits and body odor. When I've pushed my way to the pool, I have a better vantage, but still can't find him. A server with a tray full of coconut drinks asks me if I'd like one—the fourth I've been offered in the past hour, by the way—and I stiffly shake my head, smiling apologetically before continuing my private pursuit. I must really look like I need a drink.

I'm not sure what I was expecting to do anyway. Maybe I'm totally devoid of intent and, as per Scott-usual, I'm resorting to the simple satisfaction of staring at something pretty and taking mental notes for my shower later. I'm such a creep, right? And isn't that basically the same thrill as porn, boiled down? Staring at something you literally can't have, just for the mere satisfaction?

I've given up the chase already. I lean against a post and watch the pool in a trance, the noise of families and dance music flooding my ears. The moment I've given up, the odd inner excitement returns as I remind myself that I'm on a big boat full of possibilities—a boat I have yet to truly explore—and I am without the annoyance of a certain someone's company.

Suddenly, I'm elated as fuck. *Let go.* Oh, you're about to see me letting go. Need I remind myself that I'm on vacation?

Pushing into the cold hallway and taking an elevator down, I stop at the floor with all the shops. Strolling casually, I smile and let myself fill with lightness. There are so many happy faces on this boat that I find it rather refreshing. A family of four walk by the shops, and I hear the dad explain what they'll be doing for the evening, setting out their plans. When I reach the candy store, I hear a mother tell her little girl not to overdo, otherwise her appetite will be spoiled. The mother meets my eyes and she sweetly smiles, apologetic and endearing. I return her smile, touched.

In that same instant, I find a pair of parents quietly arguing. Dad doesn't want to sign up for an excursion, thinking it dangerous for their boy, while mommy argues how bad little Cory wants to do it. The boy's interested in none of it, clinging to mommy's jeans and staring off at the candy store, confused.

Is all the tension my fault? Maybe the reason Trish and Ollie are in the cabin now is because Trish hates me and Ollie is too polite to say that I'm annoying him too.

Relaxing and just "going with the flow" isn't easy for me ... but I so, so wish it was. Don't they understand? Don't they see how bad I want to be the sea?

I can fix this. It's decided. I'll return to the cabin and make up with the pair of them. That's my plan. Maybe, if I apologize in the right way and say the right things, Trish will soften up on me, Ollie will be grateful, and we'll be able to salvage this week after all.

Just when I turn to head back to the elevators, I see him. And he's *alone*.

Yes. The hot guy. The person of beautiful interest. Spotted, even despite the flashing lights and thumping music and noise. All the millions of dollars spent on making this boat gorgeous and glitzy and full of spectacle, and all my boy-obsessed ass can see is this hot guy.

With a swagger, he struts calmly along the opposite balcony to the elevators. Where's he going? Can I slip on the same elevator as him? Maybe I can strike up a convo. *He's alone*, I tell myself. *He's alone. He's available. He's there.*

What exactly do I plan to say? What should I do? Smile at him? Ask him where he's from? I'll ask what his name is; that way, I can call him something other than "hot guy".

I trip over my foot once, stumbling as I hurry to the elevators. Just when the elevators are in view, a crowd of old people block the entire width of the hall. Through blue-grey wiry hair, I catch sight of him entering an elevator. *That's my elevator! I need that elevator!* I push against the crowd as delicately and politely as I can without breaking grandma's hip. I watch as two others enter the elevator, two other people who should be me. My heart sinks as I finally break past the senior bingo club and find the glass elevator doors shut.

Standing in front of them, I watch as the hot guy peers through the glass backside, staring down at the lobby as his elevator ascends. *He doesn't see me. He's absorbed in the spectacle of the ship. I don't exist. I'll never exist to a guy like that.* Still, as he rises from view and vanishes yet again from my life, my priority quickly shifts from making up with my cruisemates to following this hottie back to the lido, which is where I suspect he's heading.

Please, don't judge me too harshly.

Since the elevators begin flooding with old people and families, I opt to take the stairs instead. That's about five flights to the lido deck where, on sore thighs and wobbly feet, I make my way through the sliding doors and into the yellow sunlight. The noise of music and the smells of chlorine and suntan lotion swarm into my nostrils, accompanied by a hint of the grill coming from the burger joint near the pool. I scope for the guy, hoping he's still on his own—and approachable. Armored with his dude-bros, I haven't a chance.

After being bumped into from behind by a fat kid with a giant tray full of chili fries, I circle the big boy pool, eyes peeled. What if he went back to his room instead? Quickly, my excitement turns to doubt, and I wonder if I should've pursued my initial desire to talk with Ollie and Trish and form the "perfect thing to say" that will put them both at ease.

When I walk past the bar, I see a sign on the wall all by itself. A little sign that reads: "Caution: deck is slippery when wet."

I stare at the sign. Are you kidding me? What sad-ass entitled fucker had to slip on a deck—surrounded by water and bearing four different swimming pools from which any of thousands of guests may take a dip—and sue the ship to warrant such a sign?

Ollie and Trish are waiting for my return. Or dreading it, I don't care. The hot guy isn't meant for me anyway. They never are.

I put on a dry-as-bone smile and make way across the deck.

And that's when my foot makes friends with the liquid remnants of someone having gotten out of the pool. My foot slips out from under me and I go face-first to the planks.

I open my eyes. By some miracle, I was able to throw my hands up fast enough to block my face from smashing into the deck. I lift my chin ever slightly, finding that I've landed at a pair of feet.

"You okay??"

"Yeah," I grunt to whomever's feet I almost kissed.

"Here, buddy. Take my hand."

I reach up blindly, grip the mystery hand and pull myself to my feet, humiliation flooding me. I look to either side, surveying the number of people whose day I've ruined as they pay shocked witness to my fall.

When my eyes meet my savior, all the blood evacuates my head screaming. My heart squeezes its way up into my ears somehow.

It's him. *Him*-him. Right in front of me. Alone. Passport line guy. White sunglasses, swagger-filled, skimpy tank. *Him*.

"You alright?" he asks again.

We're still holding hands, only now, it looks like a frozen handshake. His eyes are the deepest hazel. His button nose pinches when he smiles. A scar cuts vertically through his left eyebrow, or else that was an instruction to his barber. Even with the scanty top covering his pecs, I see the subtle bulge of them.

In front of most strangers, I would feel judged for taking so long to answer. I would get that *who-the-hell-is-this-creep* look. But from this guy, I feel none of that. I feel "interested in". I feel cared about. He waits for my answer patiently, a lopsided smile resting on his face and pushing dimples out the corner of his lips. I might, in this moment, believe I were one of his buddies he'd just helped up off the deck.

"Thanks," I finally manage to say, amidst feeling oddly breathless and my racing heart threatening to snuff out my words.

"Watch out for the slippery parts," he warns me teasingly, showing all his teeth. They aren't perfect. Somehow, that draws me in even more. *He's human, like me. He's imperfect. He's here and ... touchable.* Speaking of which, our hands are still firmly clasped. I'm not sure that I'm capable of letting go yet.

"Will do," I return, hypnotized.

For a second, he almost makes to let go of my hand—seeming like he's done with me—but an odd flicker in his eye shows otherwise. He lifts his smooth dimpled chin and squints. "You're here with another couple, right? Black guy and his girlfriend?"

I gawp. Has he seen me, too? "Y-Yes," I confirm. "My friend, Ollie. His girl, Trish."

"Ah, cool. Thought so. I remember you guys from the cruise terminal. You let my friends and I on the elevator. Saw you in the line later, too."

He noticed me. He noticed me and even remembers who I'm with. In one cursory exchange of words, he's pulled me out of the shadows and brought me to the bright and sunny world of people and awareness and interaction and wonder.

"Nice," I say numbly, omitting the fact that the *only* person I've bothered to notice on a huge ship full of countless is him. "Thanks for helping me. I'm Scott. My name is Scott."

I'm so uncomfortable. I'm in high school again and trying to sit at the cool kids' table. Why does human interaction completely elude me? The pressure paralyzes my brain. This moment has suddenly become so ... precious. The potential that lives in this chance meeting is too great to bear, rendering me stupid. Any wrongly uttered word could destroy my chance at getting to be around this beautiful guy I don't even know.

I have to figure out how to get him to like me. There's a right way to do this. There's a right way and I don't know what that is yet.

"I'm Hendry," he responds, his voice like silk sheets and velvet and everything delicious. "With a 'y'. Everyone spells it with an 'i', no idea. It's nice to meet you, Scott."

Oh, when he says my name ... Oh, oh Hendry. I'd pee my pants if my cock wasn't crammed tight as a pickle jar in these shorts.

Then our hands, still clasped, begin to move, becoming an actual handshake. My eyes dive into his, my mind racing to calculate the next amazing thing I'm going to say.

Then, quite instantly, fear fills every tip of my fingers and toes, and I blurt, "You too. Thanks again. See you around, I hope!" Then my hand drops from his and I'm off.

Off to the glass doors. *I hope he's watching.* Through them, into the ice-cold hallway. *I hope he's curious. I hope he tries to find me. I hope he gives any semblance of a shit. Please be gay.* This is the time of infinite possibilities, right?

Make this fantasy into something I can feel and touch and know as intimately as the sweat that dresses my palms.

Please let this become something more than a wish, more than just another thing to keep me up at night.

Let me experience what only the lucky and the brave have known.

Let go.

The cabin door shuts behind me, and I find Trish lying on the bed and turned away with Ollie sitting by her side stroking her hair. He looks up when I come in. He's about to say something, then reconsiders, sighing instead. I plop down on the couch and watch the TV, filled with countless possibilities of what the next seven days can behold. I forget entirely about that perfect thing I was planning to say to the pair of them. Maybe nothing needs to be said. Maybe enough has been said.

It's my next words to Hendry that need to be figured, the next time I see him. Hendry's the answer to a question I've clung to every night when I drift off to sleep. He's the sea.

[Bromosexual]

After a night on a pullout couch-bed, you'd expect me to wake up groggy. Instead, even when Trish is groaning through breakfast and complaining about the blandness of the fruit, I'm smiling and thinking about my new dream boy: Hendry. I'm going to run into him again. It's a certainty. I'm determined to get to know him, even if he's not gay. Who's to say I need a boyfriend? Present company of Ollie and Mannequin considered, maybe I'd make better memories with a totally platonic new friend.

Hendry could be that friend.

"What's got you glowing this morning?" asks Ollie. "Did you get some ass last night that I wasn't aware of?"

"I can be quiet, but I'm not *that* quiet." I chuckle, gnawing off a piece of my bacon, which Ollie watches enviously. Being on a forced cleanse with his girlfriend must suck.

What a terrible curse to cast upon a cruise.

The most of the day is spent without a care on the quiet side of the lido, lounging on the panorama deck while our Princess Plastic toasts in the sun and slurps her lemon water. I wonder if Ollie is sneaking any rogue foods past his lips when he gets a second away from her. Knowing him, I wouldn't doubt it.

Though there is a part of me that desires very much to make the most out of this ship and carefully plan our evening, I find myself so swallowed by the calm rush and pull of waves, by the distant dance music, and by the quiet chatter of nearby families, that I seem to care less and less by the second. Not to mention that my thoughts are quite clearly elsewhere, consumed in the whereabouts of Hendry. I haven't seen him on the deck yet. I don't even know which floor his cabin is, or at what end of the ship he's staying. Trust me, I've been keeping a keen lookout.

"They call them cabins," Ollie jests as we stroll along the deck, "but they're more like … oblong closets that we have to live in for a week. And there's no log fire or smores. I'm so glad we got a balcony room, dude."

"Yeah." I chuckle.

"You seem distracted." Ollie observes me, squinting. "You still pissed about Trish?"

You mean the Mannequin that's baking on a lounger somewhere? "I was never pissed." I glance over the railing, curious if Hendry or any of his buddies are down by the aft pool. They're not. "Are *you* pissed about Trish? Don't tell me this cleanse crap was your idea."

"No, no. I could use it. I could really use it. You know how many, like, chemicals go into our bodies every day? Even our shampoos are poisoning us."

I get these speeches all the time since the pair of them started dating. It's basically his girlfriend's regurgitated rhetoric which, to be fair, does him some good. He couldn't commit to any single club in high school. Ollie's changed his major twice already. It was Trish who recently got him to hone in. Maybe, in a way, she's as controlling as I am. If there's anything I could thank that rigid icicle for, it's giving Ollie some focus to his life. Not that I'd ever be caught dead admitting that to her.

Or him. "You realize you probably can't ever eat in the dining room, right?"

"I'm sure we can ask the chefs to make something that fits our ... dietary needs," Ollie insists, running his hand along the railing. "There's people who need gluten-free meals, or something free from factory-processed meats, or food that doesn't ... uh ... have things in it."

"Like a taste?" I suggest.

Ollie snorts. "It's not that bad. I feel good, honestly. Better. I have more energy when we cleanse, and my pee is less yellow."

"More info than I needed, but thanks." We come to the railing, leaning over the edge to catch the fresh breeze off the water. "You realize you can't even have butter? Ollie, dude, everything's cooked in butter."

"Not true." He says this without an actual rebuttal. Not that I expected him to have one.

The evening drops in faster than any of us were expecting, the whole day stolen out from under our sunburnt noses. Ollie and I sit on the bed while Trish occupies the bathroom, taking every minute of our patience in her long task of getting ready for dinner. It's "elegant evening" in the dining room, so my buddy and I are decked out in shirts and ties and dress slacks. Ollie's sporting a black shirt with a bright red tie. I have a white shirt I'd ironed, crisp and starched, with a diagonally striped green and black tie. I'm staring at the shine in my shoes when Ollie sighs and points out the time. I nod silently, knowing the only reason he's displaying stress about the time is for my benefit, since I'm the one who pointed out the fact that if we don't get to the dining hall by six, we're going to be waiting for a long time in the line to get in. It's half past six.

I rise off the bed Ollie and I are sitting on and double-check my hair in the mirror, ensuring each strand is in its right place. My dark head of hair is pushed forward, resting in an arrangement of gelled spikes, cropped short and tight on the sides. Everything about me is so controlled—even my hairstyle. I'm tempted to run my hands carelessly through my hair, just to defy my own desire for order, but the mere thought sends a jolt of anxiety through my chest, and I leave my perfectly arranged hair the way it is: perfectly arranged ... and in order, like a line of obedient children at school.

Trish emerges from the bathroom amidst a cloud of steam, appearing for a moment like an enormously tall drag queen from some gay 90's hell, squeezed into a skintight red dress, crimped and enormous hair up to the sky, and heels that might double as weapons. Hoop earrings dangle from her ears, and her eyes are caked with enough makeup to paint four walls of a room. She blinks twice, her gargantuan black eyelashes like two Venus flytraps, and her needle eyes hone in on Ollie. "Ready?"

"Been ready," says Ollie unhappily. He gives me a look. "Got everything you need, bud?"

"What's with the attitude?" asks Trish.

"Attitude?" Ollie gets up from the bed, circles to his girlfriend's side. "Scott made the point about us getting to the dining room at a reasonable time. Now, we'll be lucky to get our dinners by eight o' fuckin' clock."

"But I had to get ready!" she argues back, narrowing her eyes. "You took almost half an hour to shave, Ollie. You left me with no time, and the tiny bathroom was like a sauna! How am I supposed to cool off when I'm showering in a *steam* closet? I feel sweat running down my back, for fuck's sake."

"Alright, whatever. Both of you ready?" Ollie smirks, frustration in his eyes as he looks at me pleadingly.

Is he showing all this annoyance on my behalf? I shrug. "You know, maybe tonight, the line won't be so long. People stop to take pics and all that. Besides, I totally know what you mean," I say to Trish, offering her support for some ungodly pacifist reason. "I can't fathom to take another shower in that tiny bathroom without leaving the door wide open, but I'm sure neither of you care to witness—"

Trish rolls her eyes. "See?" she spits back at Ollie. "I'm not the only one. Now get my purse and let's go. I'm hungry and didn't get a chance to look at the menu."

"Lobster tail," recites Ollie from memory in a listless, bothered drone. "Mashed potatoes. Mixed veg—"

"We can't have shellfish. We can't have potatoes."

It's Ollie's turn to roll his eyes. "Mixed *vegetables*," he goes on. "All the desserts, no matter how decadent, are obviously off-limits too. Unless they're offering a head of *lettuce* as a dessert. And even then, I'm sure it'll contain some chemical we're forbidden to put in our bodies. I don't know if the mixed vegetables are fresh or come from a can, which would render *them* inedible to us as well. Seriously, Trish, why the fuck can't we do a cleanse *after* we get home? This is ridiculous."

"The amount of *poison* we put in our bodies every day is ridiculous," she fires back. "Supporting your daily activities with brain fog, fatigue-inducing chemical byproducts, and unnatural substances is ridiculous."

"Chemicals come from the earth! Every fucking thing on this planet *is* natural because every fucking thing on this planet *came* from nature! Ask the chemist," he says, throwing a hand at me. "Ask the fucking chemist."

"I'm not a chemist," I murmur quietly.

Trish swipes her red cheetah print purse off the counter and leaves the room without another word. "Trish," Ollie calls out. He goes to the door, staring after her down the hall. "Trish!" He huffs. "Mother fuckin' fuck." He lets the door close behind him in his pursuit.

I pick at my nails, listening as Ollie chases his girlfriend down the hall. The cries of her name fade and fade as he goes, and soon I'm left in just the company of the air conditioning and my own breathing. I take one deep breath, then let it all out on my hands.

That tiny moment of connection Trish and I had was rather nice, but it doesn't save me from the guilt I'm feeling that the only reason Ollie got miffed was on my behalf and my insistence on being punctual. How many of their fights have to do with me? Is that the reason Trish and I never get along? Am I like the disapproving sibling of Ollie's that Trish privately resents?

I push out the door and look for the two of them. They're gone. Out of sight and out of earshot. Maybe they'll be at the dining room. I take the glass elevator to the lobby where the entrance to the dining hall lives, then get in line, which is in fact quite fucking long. If Ollie and Trish find me, they can join me in the line. If they don't ...

Well, I guess there's worse things than eating on elegant night all by yourself. I wait patiently and scope the others in the line. Some people's idea of "elegant attire" is rather questionable, considering the arrangements of plaid and jeans and frightful boots I'm paying witness to. Welcome to the south.

I see a gaggle of teens who all look dressed up for prom teasing each other and laughing loudly as they cross the lobby and get in line right behind me. I listen to their high school banter, reminded of how Ollie and I used to be before we, y'know, *grew up*. It was only three years ago, but when you hit college, suddenly high school feels a lifetime ago. I can't even recall more than three teachers' names.

But I can still tell you the atomic number of titanium. It's twenty-two, which is likely the same number as the age I'll die. In my obituary they'll put: "Died of a poorly-planned cruise. He will be missed by all of his prescription meds and, especially, his desktop planner. In lieu of flowers, send some Xanax."

About thirty minutes later, I've reached the front of the line, and there's still no sign of either of my cruisemates. A stiff Polish lady smiles at me and, thick of accent, asks for my cabin number, which I give her. "Table for three?" she asks after looking me up in her system. "No," I say quietly. "Just the one."

I'm seated in a sea of white-cloth two-person tables with utensils arranged in perfect lines and shiny white dishes. I'm afraid to touch anything, and apparently the host can tell because she plucks my delicately-arranged cloth napkin off the table and lays it across my lap. I thank her with a squeak from my throat as she hands me the menu, then commands me to enjoy my dinner and saunters away. Or maybe she's just doing her job.

I survey the people around me, curious who I've been seated near. All the tables in my immediate vicinity are empty, giving me the feeling that I must smell, or else appear to be the sole carrier of some vicious flesh-eating disease. At my quarantine seat here in the sea of white tables, I pretend nothing is amiss and daintily peruse my menu, curious of what succulent things will be offered this night.

Despite enjoying the peace from my pair of friends, I can't deny it'd be nice to have a *little* bit of company. Even if they can't eat ninety-five percent of what the dining room is serving. I'm still looking around when the server stops by to ask if I'd like anything to drink. I ask for a tea, then choose an appetizer and main course off the menu. He takes it from my hand and disappears, leaving me to my lonesomeness once more.

I hear laughter coming from a table in the distance. The room is dim, so I can't tell if it's the teenagers that were standing behind me in line, or a family of ... what appears to be seven guys. Brothers? Cousins?

One of them turns his head.

Oh my god. It's ... It's ... What was his name? I'm affixed to him like a victim to a basilisk, turned to stone. His eyes strike me even from across the room, pinning my limp body to the chair and cruelly stealing all my breath. His head buzzed up to the top, the little waves of dirty blond hair in the front are styled lazily, parted to one side. He wears a navy suit jacket with a slight sheen to it, form-fitting, over a white shirt with a skinny black tie, cut in half by a little silver clip.

And if seeing all this isn't enough, at the sight of me, recognition dawns on him, and he smiles handsomely, his teeth flashing. He lifts a hand and gives a wave from across the room.

Me? He's ... He's waving at me? I look to my left and right, wondering if he's waving at one of his buddies from behind me. When my gaze returns to him, I find him laughing.

Then, he rises and crosses the room. I feel my eyes shrinking and my hands going all clammy. I'm suddenly unable to swallow.

He stands before me. "Hey, Scott!"

Hendry. That's his name. My brain's fogged up. Brain fog? Isn't that the term Trish used in the room? Am I all full of deadly chemicals or some shit like that?

"Hey, Hendry!" I put on a smile, my heart hammering so hard in my chest it could break. I feel my face flushing up at once, wondering if everyone in this vast room is staring at me.

"Are your friends sitting here?" he asks, tapping the other chair.

I shake my head. "N-No. Just me. They decided to ... I think they decided to dine on their own. I'm not really sure."

Hendry glances back at his buds. Not one of them seems to mind his abrupt departure. He faces me again. He shaved. His skin is smooth, revealing a tiny crescent scar that interrupts his otherwise perfect jawline. "Bro, you shouldn't be sitting all alone."

Bro. He called me bro. "Well, I don't mind it much. It's just a meal, anyway. I figured my friends could enjoy a night on their own."

"So you're all alone for dinner *and* for the rest of the night?" he asks.

Somehow, his question doesn't come off insulting, nor does it imply that he thinks I'm some sort of weirdo for flying solo on this elegant, couple-riddled night full of perfume and silky dresses and starched collars.

"Pretty much," I confess with a shrug.

"Nah. Nope. Not gonna let that happen."

He yanks out the chair and takes a seat across from me. I gawp when I realize what's happening: he's abandoned his friends simply to keep me company so that I don't have to sit alone. This fact makes me more embarrassed, like I don't deserve his kindness.

I turn that into words. "Seriously, Hendry, you don't have to—"

"Of course I don't have to. I want to. Have you ordered yet?" He yanks a napkin from an unoccupied neighboring table, lays it across his own lap. "Don't you like how there's no prices on the menus? It's so great being on a cruise with everything paid for and done for you."

Oh my god. He's talking to me and stuff. "Love it." My forehead sweats. Heat gathers under my arms. "Feel like I'm gonna go home, sit down to eat, and starve to death waiting for someone to lay a napkin over my lap."

He bursts into guttural laughter at my quip, drawing the scandalized attention of two couples by the windows. Despite the attention his laughter earned, I'm unembarrassed, noticing instead how adorable he looks. His cute button nose scrunches up, his eyes squeeze shut, his eyebrows—the one with the slit and the one without—pull in, and his face flushes red. The sound of his laughter is squeaky and boyish and deep all at once.

"Oh man, that shit's funny!" he says after he recovers, carelessly wipes his forehead with the napkin before tossing it back into his lap. "You're a funny guy! I love a sense of humor. So, tell me about you. What's your story?"

I want to know his story first. I imagine it has to do with frat houses and locker rooms and twenty girlfriends he's had throughout his formative years. He probably has a dog named Football and a shelf somewhere in his room with all his soccer trophies.

"I don't really have much of a story," I say lamely. "I want to hear yours."

"My story changes every day," he retorts, folding his arms on the table and leaning forward slightly, bringing his sharp hazel eyes into my bubble of space. I feel my heart quicken delightfully. "For instance, an hour ago, I was pretty sure this would be another boring cruise of listening to my bros yacking on about the hot girls on the ship, and doing nothing about it but lying in the sun all day turning red—*none of them tan, dude, they all just burn.* And then I see your lonely ass sitting over here, and I ask myself, 'Why is that handsome Scott fellow sitting all by himself?' Now, we're all dressed up, feeling all elegant, and I'm having dinner with that guy."

"We're having dinner?" I literally ignore the fact that he just called me handsome and, in typical Scott fashion, tend to my worries first. "But aren't you assigned over there?"

"Assigned? No idea. You ordered yet?"

"Yes. But ... they have a system in place, and they ask for your cabin number when you come in so they know where you are, and ..."

"I'll flag over the waiter-guy when I see him bring my order," he says, flipping a hand in the air for example. "His name's Yaroslav. Cute guy, has a bump for a nose."

Hendry has a good memory, and he's very observant. I find these qualities extremely erotic, somehow. In a world full of bland soup, intelligence is the spice that brings a guy like me to life.

"Cute guy?" I echo, as if just now hearing the words.

Hendry lifts his adorable eyebrows. "Oh. Am I barking up the wrong tree?"

Oh my god. I'm a tree? He's barking? Is he saying what I think he's saying? Is he asking what I think he's asking? "Do you mean ...?"

"Oh, fuck. You're straight?"

"No," I answer as fast as lightning.

Hendry sighs with relief. "Ah! Great! Had me worried there for a sec. These cruises are always so full of married couples and drunken straights making embarrassing passes at each other. Such a *relief* to run into a guy like you."

I smile at his words. Though, deep inside, doubt makes love with my throbbing heart, and I'm left wondering if he's only talking to me because I'm gay like him. Wouldn't that be the worst? To find the only other gay guy on the ship, to find that he's gorgeous as sin ... yet isn't attracted to me. He's just settling for me, as there's no other options. I'm the default.

The realization saddens me.

"What's wrong?" he asks suddenly, his face changing.

Fuck. I'm not usually this transparent. "Oh, nothing," I say, not wanting to spoil the mood, if I daresay there is a mood to spoil. "I was just ... I didn't expect to meet another gay guy so soon. Assuming you're gay and not, like, bi-curious or ... something."

"Bromosexual," he answers with a snarky grin, handsome dimples popping out from the corners of his lips. "Know what I mean, bro?" He bumps his chest twice with a fist, then gives a cheesy smile.

This is the oddest straight-wannabe gay

dude with a bro complex I've ever met. Maybe the only one. A one-of-a-kind. I find myself unable to hold back a chuckle of amusement, my face going red for an entirely different reason. I hate how I blush so easily. No matter how I feel about being Hendry's "default", I can't help how unfathomably attractive I find him, even with his little flaws—the imperfect teeth, the vertical cut in his eyebrow, the scar at his jawline.

Just then, two of his buddies call out his name. The server's brought their food. Hendry gives a wave and says, "I've relocated! I'll take my snail mail over here, please!" He faces me, excited. "You ever had escargot? They taste like cheesy mushrooms, which is kinda gross, but hey, you only live once."

"Wow." I glance at the server, who appears confused for a minute until he realizes the change in seating arrangement. I worry if Hendry's caused a problem in the kitchen with moving to my table. Won't they have to do something in their system? I hate all this extra attention drawn to me. Really, I hate ever drawing attention to myself. "Do you ... Do you think that they'll—"

"Oh! My tea!" Hendry gets up from the table suddenly, races back to his own, and swipes his glass of tea from it. He gives one of his buds a pat on the back, winks, then returns to my table slurping on the tea. He sets it down and moans. "Best fucking tea ever. It even tastes good unsweetened, dude. How do they do that?"

My hands, sweaty as amphibians, haven't left my lap for a solid five minutes. I only now realize I'm wringing them. "Cruise magic."

"Cruise magic." He gazes into my eyes for a moment, seemingly lost in a thought. I feel instantly self-conscious, wondering if there's something on my face. Then, just as quick, the self-consciousness is replaced with an act of gazing of my own: gazing into his rich, hazel eyes that fill my vision like sticky sweet caramel, trapping me.

"I think it's just a mix," I say suddenly.

He lifts his eyebrows, the trance broken for a second. "Hmm?"

"The tea. I saw an employee filling one of the machines on the lido deck. He was pouring from a box-jug-thing."

"Ruin the magic, why don't you?" Hendry gives me a wink, then leans back as the server approaches, setting a tiny circular plate of six escargot arranged hexagonally in front of him, and a Caesar salad in front of me. "Thanks, Yaro, buddy!"

The server, Yaroslav, handsome and very cute in his vest and shaved head, gives a curt smile and nod, then tells us to enjoy our meal before sauntering off. He didn't seem too put-off by the seating change. "Accommodating," I remark, mostly to myself.

Hendry heard. "I think he's Ukrainian. I play a guessing game. Without looking at their nametags, I try to guess where they're from. Fun fact: less than four percent of the staff on this ship is American."

"Really?"

"So tell me about you." Hendry loudly slurps one of the escargot—which really do look like cheese-topped mushrooms—past his lips, which I only seem to notice just now. I can't believe I haven't noticed how sexy his lips are. Maybe it's the way he moves them, manipulating them as he eats. "You're here with your buddy and his girlfriend?"

"Best friend since childhood, really. We met in a computer lab in second grade. The computers were really crappy, but Ollie's sort of a genius with technology, and he was able to hack through to the operating system."

"Oh! You're a pair of rebel bad-asses!"

"Wouldn't go that far." I laugh. "We weren't editing grades or anything. In fact, we were programming games. Quick Basic stuff. Total nerds, the pair of us. Then we grew up and got too cool for all that in middle school. High school was our time, but when college came around, we went to separate schools. There was a really intensive program that I wanted to pursue, and Ollie preferred to stay local. I miss him, but we keep in touch regularly via Skype and Facebook and all that. College is pretty scary to go about alone."

"Life in general, bro. We can't do all this alone. We need people. Not even in a romantic sense. Just in a, like ... 'Hey, man. Life sucking for you? Awesome, me too.' It's important for us to share our mutual suckage." Hendry grins and bites his lip. "Life's not suckin' today, though, I'll tell you that much."

"Nice cruise so far?" I return the smile. "Anyway, Ollie's a bit into computers still, and I guess so am I, but we're not hacking any credit card databases or anything. He started out in business, then switched majors to science—which is what I study—and now he's an engineering major. Fickle ass dude. His girlfriend Trish probably won't let him trade majors again." I scoff privately to myself.

"Not fond of the girlfriend?"

Again. So fucking transparent tonight. I doubt I could hide a single emotion from crossing my face. Does he see my complete and utter adoration for him? Does he see my emotional and intellectual boner I got for him? Not to mention the physical one I'd have, if he touches me the right way. Or at all.

"I respect her," I answer, choosing my words carefully. "I have no reason to dislike her. Our personalities clash, perhaps. Not sure why she bugs me so much, but I respect her."

Hendry's helped himself to three more escargot while I've been talking, and he's pierced a fourth one with his fork when he responds. "I learned once that when you find yourself stuck with a dislike for someone, stop and gently pull up a big ol' mirror. What you are *actually* feeling is recognition, because that quality you hate so much about the other person is, in fact, a quality that you dislike in yourself. I spent my whole childhood fighting with my brother, and I always resented how quickly he'd give up on things. We'd play a video game, and he'd give up after dying once. The second he started losing, he'd give up. I hated that about him *so fucking much*. Until one day, my watch broke—it was a gift from my brother on my sixteenth birthday—and I caught myself in a moment of exasperation when I couldn't fix it easily, giving up and not wanting to replace it. I committed to fixing that watch, and I wear it to this day." He lifts his wrist, flashing the black leather cuff with a clock face embedded in it. It shines in the gentle candlelight glow of the dining room. "Commitment. Kinda ironic, because just a few years after that, my brother made two of the biggest commitments of all: he married a lovely lady named Becky, got her pregnant, then joined the Army."

I still haven't touched my salad, so pulled into his story that I've forgotten entirely where the hell I am. "It's a cool watch. Was clearly worth the time to fix."

"Pretty cool as fuck, huh?" He observes it, twisting his wrist to get a look, then smiling fondly. He brings his hazel eyes back to me. "Anyway, not suggesting you go and make kissy-kissy make-up with Trish or anything."

I chuckle. "Yeah, that'll never happen."

"Glad you got your buddy Ollie, though. We all need buddies. Most of my friends I made in college. Including all the fools I'm with. Some of them are coworkers." He gives a glance at them over his shoulder, then chuckles. "Coworkers from three different jobs. I'm such a bird. Commitment, right?" He gives me a look, flashing his pretty eyes, then pops the last escargot into his mouth.

Commitment. I wonder if his same love-hate for commitment and giving up applies to his relationships. I take up my fork and poke my salad, allowing myself a first bite. The taste is tangy and *perfect*, as if Caesar were being stabbed all over again by his disloyal friends in my mouth. Their daggers are tasty.

"Glad I got Ollie too," I remark while chewing, staring and considering a crouton at the end of my fork. They're just the worst. You can hardly stab them with a fork, and when you scoop them up instead, they roll right off and dive back into the salad.

"I'm still picturing you two as kids at the computers," says Hendry, giggling, "hacking into the school database and setting off the fire alarms. Old crappy computers, you said? Was it the late 90's?" When I nod, Hendry giggles. "Just a guess at your age. I was right."

"Yeah?"

"Twenty-one?" he asks, to be sure.

I take another forkful of salad and murder Caesar all over again. "For two more days."

You'd think I just told him my cock's made of gold and I poop winning lottery tickets. "HOLY CRAP!" Hendry cries out, his adorable face shattering into excitement. "Bro! We need to celebrate! Like, tonight!"

I can't help but chuckle. It's a bizarre combination of feeling like half the dining room is looking at us, as well as knowing that the convention of acting like mature adults and behaving according to the expectations of "elegant evening" is being completely ignored by the hot guy who's taken a seat at my table. I'm caring less and less by the second. I am strangely euphoric and free to do whatever I want in Hendry's company.

Apparently, it is everyone's desire to order the lobster tail on elegant night, because we both find we've ordered the same main course, along with what appears to be nearly everyone in the dining room. Elegant night shall forever be known as sucks-to-be-a-lobster night. Over our (very delicious!) shellfish, we banter back and forth about fun and not-so-fun times we had at our respective high schools. He tells me about a time he was almost beat up by two dudes *and* their girlfriends because he was mistaken for someone on the football team. "I still don't know what the fuck the *actual* guy from the football team did," he explains with a nervous laugh. I tell him about a time I almost acquired a girlfriend after a misunderstanding and a game of spin-the-bottle in eighth grade. Hendry finds that story so funny, he almost spits out his bite of lobster, then has to excuse himself with a gulp of tea. He drinks *so much* tea and water. Oddly, I find watching him gulp-gulp-gulp and observing his Adam's apple bobbing up and down very erotic. He makes art from just the use of his mouth.

I promise, I don't mean that as dirtily as it sounds. I'm not picturing his mouth doing anything else. I'm really truly, truly not.

I think.

"Ready to get out of here?" he asks after dessert, which I won't even talk about because I'm certain I've consumed six trillion calories in just the space of this past hour alone.

We leave the dining room and, in lieu of taking the glass elevators, circle up the stairs of the lobby. One of the hired musicians plays a cover of a feely Elton John classic on guitar in the lobby, his soft and sultry voice filling the whole belly of the ship. Passing along the balcony tossing stories and quips back and forth, I feel like I'm in someone else's proud, fortunate body, strolling along in someone else's dress shoes. There isn't a single thing that could convince me that I am Scott Berringer, not tonight.

Except for the fact that I keep checking my hands, as if I'm afraid they're too sweaty. Not that I'm expecting Hendry to suddenly reach out and grab one. We're not boyfriends. I don't even think he likes me that way; he's just keeping me company. Two homos finding each other in a sea of heteros.

Drifting by, we make a game of guessing how long the older couples have been married. One nine-hundred-year-old woman at the bar sports a blood red shawl and skintight gown. "That's Bessie," Hendry decides, naming her on the spot, "and Bessie is definitely getting some ass tonight." Further down the hall near the casino, he points out an old man in a long-tailed coat and top hat. "That's Jim," says Hendry, making up the story as he goes, "and he's hoping his wife doesn't find out about the ass *he's* going to be getting tonight."

The feel of his lips at my ear each time he has something funny or adorable to say sends a shiver of delight through my body. I would not mind if he had a hundred different things to say, if it meant a hundred different ticklish whispers at my ear.

"The woman at the bar in the blue sparkly thing," I say back, playing his game. "That's Nanette, and she's cougaring all over that teen Prom King standing next to her."

"Hmm, that's probably her son," he says back, studying them.

"I suck at this game."

We end up at a piano bar just beyond the casino, seated on barstools side by side at a round bar that surrounds a lifted piano, at which another hired man plays tunes and heckles the crowd for their bad requests. Hendry tosses a five dollar bill at the piano and shouts, "Play some Nirvana!" The man grins, because the greasy green language of money speaks louder than elegance and thick perfume, and we're soon treated to a classical version of *Heart-Shaped Box*.

As the man sings and Hendry and I spend a moment to listen to the song, our elbows graze one another's on the counter. My heart jumps, feeling the contact. I feel a strange, uncharacteristic courage in me. Do I dare acknowledge our elbows touching? Slowly, ever slowly, I give my elbow a little push.

He responds, pushing back a bit. As subtle as a spy, I give a quick glance at his face out of the corner of my own, only to find that he's watching me with a playful smirk. My face goes red, my pulse welcomes itself to my ears, and I return my attention to the piano, all the nervousness rushing back in an instant. Every little moment with him is like a first date.

I'm so fucking out of practice. The only lover I've ever really had is my right hand, and we're very well-acquainted. Attached, even. I feel so sensitive to his every touch and breath. Vulnerable as a kitten in the wild, shuddering at every little noise. Hendry's the big bad wolf, sniffing me out, watching me, grinning with all his teeth and looking sexy as hell. He can pick his nose and make it look sexy. He can scratch his ass, belch up lobster butter and escargot, or take a leak at a urinal. I'm certain anything that Hendry does, he does looking as sexy as a dream.

I've never wanted anyone so bad. And I don't even know what I want to do to him. Or what he'd do to me. I'm like a virgin.

"Madonna," I say, tossing my own five dollar bill, and the man plays *Like A Virgin.*

Afterwards, when we pass down the main hall that connects shops, lobby, and casino to the other end of the ship, we find it caked from end to end with photographers and their backdrops. Knowing it's all just another way to make money off us, just like the incessant pushing and selling of alcohol, I shake my head and wave one off when he encourages us to take a picture, but Hendry has other plans.

"Fuck yeah, you can take our pic!" Hendry exclaims, and despite my protests, he pulls me in front of a backdrop full of amber sunsets and crashing waves on a beach. The eager photographer, taking us to be just another pair of buddies, suggests some manly pose for us to do. Hendry takes one look at me, then says,

"Need some saving tonight, princess?" Before I can stop him, Hendry's grabbed me into his arms like some fucking damsel in distress that he rescued from an ivory tower, and with me laughing in his arms and him grinning down at me from his dashingly handsome height, the photographer catches the moment in five bright flashes. The only thing that exists in this moment is Hendry's rich eyes and his lopsided, toothy grin, and the joyful feeling of my body hanging helplessly in his arms.

I have never felt more freed from a tower than I do right now.

There's still a hundred different things we could do within the bowels of the ship, but Hendry takes me up to the panorama—the ring of deck just above the lido. It's nearly ten o'clock at night, and the sky and sea is pure black. We stroll side by side along the railing, our hands occasionally brushing past one another. I pretend not to notice, playing it cool despite my heart sending all these alerts and panic alarms of delight to my brain. The ship looks like it's sailing along the stars with no gulf beneath it at all. The effect is almost scary as we eerily drift through the nothingness, wind pushing past our faces. I feel so far away from home, from work, from school, from everything and everyone I know.

Alone with a stranger named Hendry. A stranger who, by the minute, becomes less and less strange. Yet still, an untimely wave of homesickness strikes me in the chest. Maybe it's just my natural defensive reaction to experiencing so much newness in such a short amount of time. I suddenly feel scared, like I want to do something to comfort myself: rush under a blanket, or put myself to bed, or check my fucking email.

"You alright?"

I look up from my daze, nearly having forgotten where I am. "Yeah, I'm great," I tell him, insisting perhaps a bit too much. "Was just noticing how eerie the boat looks at night, floating out here in the middle of ... in the middle of ..."

"Looks like a spaceship, doesn't it? Give your eyes some time to adjust," he says, then points upwards. "You'll start to see more and more stars. Constellations, even."

I look up. All I see is black, black, black.

He stops and rushes up to the railing. I'm given a little gift of his backside when he does. His tight-fitting blue blazer hugs a bit at his shapely ass. I fight an urge to squeeze it.

Slowly, I draw up to his side. Strategically, I make sure to come quite close to him, close enough for our elbows to kiss. Even through the fabric of my shirt and his blazer, there is electricity in our every touch. I hope he feels it too. This can't all just be in my little lonely, hungry head.

"It's like dust," he murmurs.

His mouth doesn't need to be by my ear. Just his little words send a message through the network of my body, from my ear, down the cable of my neck, down my spine, jiggling me everywhere in my belly, sending an email alert to my cock, then wrestling its way down my thighs and converting my knees into noodles. How the fuck does he do that?

I turn my face and study the side of his as he stares into the endless black unknown. The crashing sound of waves as the cruise ship cuts through the gulf is all we hear. I'm with him. He's with me. No one is around. We're alone.

We're alone.

I stare and I stare at him. I want to kiss him. I keep daring myself to do it. Do it. *Do it.*

Let go.

"Just blackness and nothing," he murmurs, turning into a philosopher. "Nothing ..."

A philosopher.

Let go. Fucking do it.

"I've never been one to believe in fate," he says, "but sometimes ..."

Kiss him. He's only a touch taller than you. Reach up and put your lips against his smooth, beautiful face. Taste him. *Taste him.*

"Sometimes too many good things happen all at once. And it's my natural instinct to wonder, like ..." He searches for his words while I search for the courage to carry out my own dare. "When is my lucky streak gonna end? When is fate gonna fuck me up? ... Know what I mean?"

He turns his face to me, finds me staring at him with my hungry, yearning intent. My pulse has relocated to my eyeballs. Literally, his face flashes with my every heartbeat. It's possible I could be going into cardiac arrest.

"Know what I mean?" he repeats, quieter.

I heard his words. I know what he means, but I'm not in the mood for philosophy. I don't believe in fate. I believe in chemistry. I believe in choices. I believe in cause and effect and I don't believe in chance meetings.

Then, words happen. "I don't believe in fate, Hendry."

He smiles gently, comforted somehow by my words. "I like you, Scott. Whether it's by fate or just for the fun of it, I'm glad you slipped in that puddle and crashed into me."

I smile back. I don't want him to call it a night yet. I'm not sure exactly what I want, as

I'm afraid some instant bang-bang in one of our rooms would cheapen whatever this is that we've created. I don't even think either of our rooms is an option anyway, considering our company. I don't even know if it's my priority anymore to kiss him. I just ... I just ...

I just want to be around him and I never want this night to end.

"I'm getting kinda tuckered out," he says.

The dreaded words. We're parting ways. My heart splits in half and all my opportunity to do *anything* with him has just been robbed from me. "Oh. Really?"

"Tomorrow's the first port day. I think we dock at, like, seven or eight. Is Jamaica where we're stopping first? Or ... Cayman Islands?"

Lonely blue ball hell. That's where we're stopping. "Montego Bay, Jamaica," I answer.

"Ah, right. That's the one. My buddies got an excursion and I gotta get ready with them and all that. Friends can be so inconvenient, am I right?" He gives me a grin. "Hey. You got any excursions planned?"

Trish is afraid of fish, stingrays, dolphins, and anything else remotely interesting. Ollie thinks hiking is lame, but mentioned being interested in the bus ride downtown—until Trish expressed fear of Jamaican locals, citing two cases she read about in which tourist buses were robbed at gun point. Ollie and I discussed snorkeling in the Caymans back when I didn't know Trish was joining us, but we never signed up, and now clearly we won't.

But I don't care about excursions anymore. I'll happily spend my seven days hanging out with Hendry doing next to nothing at all. It's been so long since I've felt closeness with a guy. In all honesty, have I *ever* truly felt this sort of intimacy? Is this my first time? I don't even care if Hendry and I never get romantic. I crave his companionship. I know, I know. We just met. We've only tonight begun to learn a bit about each other, but in the vacuum of close male relationships that I've had in my life, is it so weird to crave this that badly? Starve a guy half his life, then dangle the tastiest bit of meat before his lips ... how can you blame him for snapping his jowls?

"You alright?"

I look up. I realize I haven't answered his question. "We didn't plan any excursions. It's Ollie's girlfriend. She's sort of difficult. She's afraid of everything that has a pulse. And Ollie's bored of everything that doesn't."

"Maybe they'll change their mind when they see other people doing all the fun stuff and making it back with all their limbs still intact." Hendry smiles. "Wanna grab some ice cream before we call it a night?"

I swallow all my babyish whininess and put on a smile, determined to enjoy myself. "Only if they have chocolate!"

"Race you there."

Suddenly, he bolts away. Running? On a somewhat dark deck that could be slippery?

Fuck it. *You only live once*, or some shit like that. I tear after him. I might trip racing him down the stairs to the ice cream machines by the pool, but I run.

His laughter echoes off the deck chairs and the wooden planks and the glass.

I don't trip and fall on my face.

When we get to the machine, we wait for a cluster of kids to finish, listening to them scream and chirp and make fun of one another. Hendry gives me a look, and I return it with a remark: "To be young and careless again."

"We *are* young," he answers back. "Even when we're sixty. We'll be listening to the same music. We'll be tasting the same ice cream. We'll be hacking computers and calling each other up to laugh about the good times."

"In other words," I add, "we're gonna be cool as fuck when we're grandpas."

"Just as cool as fuck as we are now, bromo! Guaranteed."

Hendry serves himself a vanilla from the soft serve dispenser. I get myself a chocolate in those little squared-off wafer cones that taste like cookie cardboard. Sauntering across the emptied deck, we eat our respective ice creams in a peaceful silence. He keeps catching me staring at him, and each time I look away like an idiot, a heavy metal drummer inviting himself into my central nervous system.

He shoves the last bite of wafer into his sexy-when-it-moves mouth. "I'll catch you sometime tomorrow, Scott!"

"Looking forward to it," I reply, half my ice cream still left to eat.

We part ways at the glass elevators. When I get back to my room, I find Ollie and Trish already asleep in the joined pair of beds. For a second, I think they're both asleep, but then I see Ollie's eyes part—the glint of them visible through the darkness—and his eyes seem to smile. Whether it's just a smile of greeting, or a smile to assure me that things are okay between them, I don't know. I just pop the rest of the ice cream into my mouth, then slip into the bathroom.

I change into something more comfy, but I take my time. I take my time because I'm pretending it's Hendry who's undressing me.

I close my eyes.

He's there, waiting for me at the backs of my eyelids. *"Looking sexy, Scott. Take the rest off for me. Show me what you got."* I let my pants slip to my ankles. I pull off my tie and shrug my dress shirt to the floor. *"Show me it all,"* he says, drawing close. *"Let go."*

My eyes open, and I'm still gripping my shoes. I'm naked, and still can't let go.

[I am Not An Easy Tail]

When we return from the duty free shops at the port, we set ourselves up at a table by the windows and have lunch on the lido. Ollie says a word or two and the Mannequin just stares at the plain storefront and a pair of drummers seated on the concrete, drumming for tips. That's what Mannequins do best: sit and look pretty. Though she nibbles on a fruit salad and hides silently behind sunglasses that cover half her face, I wouldn't say she looks upset about anything, but rather trapped in some curious, complex thought that I can't decipher. Ollie seems just the same, tiredness in his eyes as he looks the opposite way, staring at a bunch of kids chasing each other in circles around the pool.

Next time you're on a little vacay and any part of you is feeling blue or grossly unfilled, remind yourself of this: behind every smile you see is a miserable soul trying to convince his or herself that they're happy. Don't be fooled for one weak minute; they are, all of them, desperate for a rescuing.

Hendry rescued me, but I haven't seen him all day. I glance through the window and imagine him in Jamaica doing something super cool. Hiking a big trail with his buddies. Laughing too hard at a joke one of them says. Snorkeling in some skintight lycra outfit.

And I'm … not. I sip my lemonade and wince as the breeze brushes through my hair.

"You two okay?" I ask Ollie when Trish has gone to refill her glass of water.

"We are super," he answers, piddling with a fork he used to eat his own salad, and not seeming as though he'd wish to discuss it if something *were* wrong.

I let him have his space. To be honest, I'm too occupied in my own misery, feeling as if every minute of my day is a waste that isn't spent with Hendry. I'd almost resent how my thoughts of him consume me so completely if I didn't enjoy his company so much.

When Trish plants herself in a deck chair the way a long-legged spider nestles itself in a web, Ollie does a good job of distracting me from my brain fog (I'm going to use that term all the time now, just because.) by pulling me with him to the gym. To be honest, even with all my research, I've completely neglected to notice the gym onboard. Ollie and I occupy a set of treadmills, and the hypnotic thrumming of footfalls and grinding of rubber fills our brains. We are so happy not to talk about a single damn thing for a while.

And then: "So what'd you do last night?"

I flinch, my attention pulled from the little movie on the monitor attached to the machine. "What? Last night? Oh ..." I shrug. We've been running long enough that I don't even feel the burn in my thighs anymore. I'm so out of shape. "I ate in the dining room."

"I'm so fucking hungry, man."

"I know."

"Fucking cleanse." Ollie runs the length of his arm across his forehead, which only seems to trade the sweat of his face with the sweat of his arm. "Feel like I'm gonna collapse."

"Don't push yourself." I look at him, taking the role of annoying-concerned-friend. I happen to be an expert. "You need to keep hydrated and keep your energy up. I don't want to have to carry you down to the clinic. I read this one review, and they said it's, like, miserable and windowless and ... *stark*."

"Alright," he says, coming to a stop, tapping a button, then pulling himself off the machine and sitting on its edge. I do the same. "Tell me about this delicious elegant food I missed last night. Make me super fucking jealous. Do your worst, Scott."

"Lobster. Buttery. Caesar salad." Quite suddenly, I'm touched by last night's memory. It feels so far away, and it was just last night. I almost question whether it happened at all. Maybe it's someone else's memory. Maybe I dreamt it all.

"And ...?"

I smile. "And a guy named Hendry."

"Who?"

"Hendry." I already feel myself blushing.

Ollie's eyes flash. "You met a dude? For real?"

"I slipped and fell into him. Then he sorta ran into me in the dining room and ... well ..."

I can't remember the last time I talked to Ollie about a guy, but it never feels any more comfortable than the last. I came out to him my freshman year of high school, mostly because that was about the time I admitted it to myself. Ollie didn't give a crap, which made me think he already had his suspicions.

When I finish telling him the story, minus an awkward detail or two, Ollie slaps me on the back. "About time. You need me to, like, give you the room one of these nights or ... or something? Can you do your business on the couch? Because, like, I'm not sure I can sleep in the bed afterwards if, like—"

"No, no, no." I laugh, which makes my eyes explode. My nose tingles and my cheeks are on fire. "It's not like that. No. I mean, like, *maybe* something will happen. I don't know. But I'm not, like ... I'm not going to take him back to the room and do the busy-busy-bang-bang. I don't even know how. I've been single so long, I feel like I'm in a relationship with my right hand and gotta ... reconcile things and make decisions. I don't even know if he likes me in that way. At least, not officially."

"You know you're a good-looking guy."

I stare at Ollie, red-faced and all.

"Seriously," he says, as if annoyed by my dubiousness. "You can't deny all the girls who were into you. Even Trish thinks you're hot."

"Trish can't stand me."

"Trish also can't stand you. But you're still hot, man. This Henry guy would be a fool if he wasn't, like, into you or whatever."

"Hendry. With a 'd'."

"Weird name."

"Unique." I smile, thinking on his flashy smile and that tiny dash in his eyebrow and how his button nose scrunches up cutely when he grins or laughs. "It's unique."

"Maybe we can do a double date thing. I feel like it's the thing we all need. It'll make Trish happy. It'll take the focus off *me* and *my* flaws, for once. And—"

"So something *is* up with you guys?"

Ollie rolls his eyes, caught. "I didn't say that. How about dinner tonight? The menu looked Trish-friendly."

"Well. If I can find him. And if he's up for it and ... and doesn't have plans or something. I don't want to call it a double date. Like I said, I really don't know if he's—"

"Double date it is," he decides.

Ollie gets up, suddenly invigorated, and heads for the weight machines. My heart feels light in an instant, motivated more than ever to find Hendry, wherever the hell he is.

The day crawls by ever slowly, minute by excruciating minute. Ollie eventually joins his girlfriend to bake in the sun, and I'm left wandering the ship and watching over the railing as grouping by grouping of people return from their misadventures in Montego Bay. The musicians have been since traded for a very loud pair of men who are dressed up in marching band attire and pump trumpets and snare drums as loud and proud as a football halftime show. Even from the height of approximately one trillion stories, I watch their tiny ant shapes as they make their music.

As if I'll recognize Hendry from way up here.

A handful of hours later, the boat has already set sail for its next destination, and I'm leaning on the railing of the panorama scoping the lido deck below for a certain someone. *How can he not be anywhere?* Like some obsessed crazy person, I consider if he got injured in Jamaica on his excursion with the guys. Or maybe they went overtime and missed getting back on the ship. Or maybe they got accosted by the people Trish read about. Literally a hundred things are going through my head, and not one of them is nice.

"We should just go to dinner," I tell them an hour later when the three of us are back in the room. "I don't know where he is."

Trish looks unimpressed, sitting on the bed in a skintight white thing. Even Ollie looks a little tired of waiting, and he gives a careless shrug, then says, "Sure, man. Maybe another night."

We eat dinner together in the dining hall for the first time this cruise. The hostess lays a napkin across each of our laps, which oddly seems to amuse Trish, who lets out a giggle. I wasn't until now aware that she's capable of giggling.

I don't see Hendry the rest of the night.

"Any plans for the Caymans tomorrow?"

Ollie asks this as we pass by the casino, much to Trish's chagrin. "Fucking smoke," she says derisively, sneering at the clouds and demonstratively coughing as we go.

"There's a lot more area to walk around, from what I hear," I point out, trying so hard to keep my spirits up despite the utter lack of the *one* person I want to see. "A lot more shops and stuff. Very pretty, what I heard. Chickens running along the streets like they have no care in the world. But you have to be careful, because—"

"Always be *careful*," says Trish mockingly. "Look out for this. Watch out for that. Don't you ever get sick of yourself?"

I stop, giving her a glare. "I'm serious. I read online—"

"Yeah, I read things online too. Y'know, I'm pretty sure your Harris guy's found another fling and he's giving him the nasty in his bunk right now."

The blow is low, stinging, and cold.

"Fuck you, Trish."

"Whoa, whoa." Ollie gets between us, as if we're actually going to unsheathe blades and make at one another's throats out in the open.

"Seriously," she says, utterly unmoved by my profanity. "Why make a big deal over this guy? It's a cruise. People take cruises and they find themselves some easy tail, and if you're not easy enough, they move on. I have gay friends. I know how it works."

"It wasn't like that with us," I say, utterly unmoved by her insinuation that gay guys' priorities are all about getting ass. "It was ... It was fucking different. We connected."

"Magical," she remarks with a flip of her hair and an acid smirk.

I walk away. I don't listen to Ollie as he calls out my name. Three times. I make for the elevators, entirely finished with the presence of couples and smoke and chatter and other human beings having fun. Approaching the glass elevators, I'm reminded of that moment on my first day when I desperately tried to get on the same elevator as Hendry. I didn't even know his name. I hadn't yet fallen to his feet.

The elevator carries me up the throat of the beast, and when I empty onto the lido deck, it's already nightfall. There's a movie playing on a giant screen above the pool, giving a ghostly glow to all the people spread across the deck chairs watching. In a heat of emotion, I just tramp to the first empty one I can find and plop myself into it. The damn thing is wet, soaking through my pants and the sexy pair of underwear I picked out for tonight. Here is my empty hand, and upon it, the amount of fucks I give.

The movie makes me sleepy. I turn on my side, cuddling a towel I'm not sure is mine. The boat rocking so subtly that only the very keen can tell, I turn my eyes from the endless black that is the sky and let myself drift away. Doesn't matter, I still can't see the stars.

[The Unlisted Excursion]

I spot Hendry in the Caymans perusing a kiosk of sunglasses across the street.

Ollie points at a store with seashells in the front, and as he and Trish disappear into it, I split from them and make way across the road. A car I didn't notice screeches to a halt and I pay it no mind. Someone shouts something at me in another language, but I'm pursuing the boy at the sunglasses stand.

He's trying some on when he notices me.

"Hey, bromo!" he exclaims behind a pair of white sunglasses with a sharp red line along its rim.

"Missed you yesterday," I blurt, unable to help myself. I know. We've known each other for, like, a day, and I'm already breaking the gay rules of coming off too clingy and emo and all that. I feel one step away from giving him the WHERE WERE YOU?! speech, like I have the right.

"How do these look?" He turns his head left, turns it right. He's wearing a loose-fitting red tank and bright white board shorts, and the glasses couldn't match him better if he tried. Maybe he did try. "Only ten dollars!"

"Cayman dollars, or U.S.?" I ask back, studying the selection of shades myself. I pull a sleek black pair with red lenses to examine, but wouldn't dare touch it to my nose. Does he even *know* how many grimy, greasy faces have touched these?

"Totally didn't see you yesterday," he says after pulling off the shades. "Looked for you."

My heart jumps into my throat and my eyes flash widely. "Really?"

"The excursion took us all damn day. Then, when we got back on the ship, Ray had this bad cramp in his stomach—he's always been such a wuss—and Jase and I stayed with him for a couple hours in his room before calling the medic. Either he ate something bad, or he's having his first period. I feel sorry for him either way."

"That sucks." I try to fit that image into my awful day yesterday. Him, tending to an ailing friend while I was in the dining room sulking like a child with my best friend and a plastic Barbie. Why do I always assume the worst?

Oh. Dinner. Double date. We'd wanted to do it yesterday, but ... "Hey, by the way," I blurt. "If you're ... uh, open to the idea ... I was thinking maybe we could, uh ..." I'm suddenly full of doubts and naggings. What if he has plans tonight already?

"Yeah?" he says, prodding, his eyes alight.

Get it out, you wuss. "Wanna join me and my friends for d-dinner tonight?"

"Fuckin' love to," he answers right away.

My insides explode with relief. My cock jumps twice in my tight shorts. I might've just soiled them too. I'll keep these observations to myself.

"Great!" I exclaim. "Six o'clock sound like a plan?"

"Sure." Hendry smiles. The sun paints his face in a brilliant, healthy shade of bronze, his hair made golden and all the dirtiness washed from his blond buzzed sides and messy waves on top. "I have no idea where my buddies are. They kinda left me back here. You wanna join us now? Or ..."

Before I can say yes, I hear my name shouted from across the street. I turn to find Ollie and Trish standing on the opposite curb, questions in their eyes.

Thanks, mom and dad. Don't they see me with this gorgeous guy? Can't they put two and two together and realize this is Hendry?

Ollie gives a lazy sort of expectant wave, as if beckoning me and saying hello at the same time.

"Ah, you're here with your friends. Ollie and Trish, right?" It's so strange to hear those names in Hendry's silky, inviting voice. "That them?" He waves back, as if the wave were intended for him. Ollie freezes, unsure what to do. Trish folds her arms and lifts her shades, as if to get a better look.

I'm just not ready for Hendry to meet them. I didn't expect all this to happen in the middle of the streets in the Cayman Islands.

"I better get back to them," I say, putting the shades back on the stand. I'd love nothing better than to spend the day with Hendry and his buddies. There's about a million and a half fantasies I could fulfill among them, and most of those fantasies aren't even sexual. "I'll see you tonight at six in the lobby, then?"

"Tonight at six," Hendry agrees. He slaps the side of my arm, the sting discharging a bolt of pleasure through me. "Later, bromo!"

Hendry takes his glasses to the vendor, pulling out his wallet, and I turn and—with a touch more caution this time—cross the road to meet my friends again. Funny, how I seem to abandon all sense of worry when my motive is pursuing Hendry. I wonder if he's the secret antidote to my curse ... the silver to my wolf, the garlic-butter seasoning to my vampire.

"Is that the Henry guy?" asks Ollie when I've returned.

Ugh. It's Hendry. "He agreed to dinner at six," I tell them. Then, snidely, I half-turn my face to Malibu Barbie. "Please don't humiliate me in front of him. I really like this one."

Trish is still studying him with her shades lowered. "He's hot," she observes dryly.

Somehow, her compliment feels more like a warning. I disregard it. "Did you guys find anything in the store?"

"T-shirts about drunk frogs and magnetic beer bottle openers that have boobs on them," Ollie answers.

Every store. "Great. Let's keep on."

Keep on, we do. The Caymans are a much improved experience after the chance meeting. Is that all we are, Hendry and I? A series of chance meetings? I suppose being on a cruise has its social benefits: you meet and run into the same people over and over again. Funny, how I seem to not recognize nor give half a fuck about a single other entity on the boat full of thousands. The effect of meeting Hendry was, apparently, that powerful.

The ship finds us a few hours later bearing a bag full of cheap purchases of souvenirs for friends and family back home, including a shot glass for my collection. "You hardly ever drink," Trish says, criticizing my desire to collect shot glasses. *And you hardly ever eat*, I want to quip back, but there's a thing called "self-discipline" that I'm trying to exercise.

The cruise ship roars back to life at four o'clock in the afternoon, but I'm not on the deck to see it off this time. I'm already in the room picking out my clothes for the evening while Trish and Ollie return to the deck.

Alone in the room and feeling the rumble of the ship's engine beneath my feet and the slow twist of the ship pulling from the dock, I nurse a sunburn on my neck, frustrated with myself for not having worn more sunscreen. Whether I got it at the Caymans or Jamaica or both, I don't know. I have to remember to wear more in Cozumel, our final port tomorrow.

Already, my vacation's more than halfway over. Four days, has it been? I can't even tell the proper day of the week. Time is irrelevant on the ship. Even space. It's strange to process that we're on what can basically be likened to a floating city in the gulf, so my brain doesn't quite process that we've left Galveston and have touched the sands of more than one country. Part of me feels like I'm still in Galveston, still excitedly anticipating my vacation. Part of me feels like I still haven't left my apartment in Austin, worrying about that one thing I forgot to pack.

Maybe I'll never leave my dry little home. Maybe I'm stuck in the safety of it forever.

After I've showered and put on my tight, sexy underwear, the pair of jeans that are soft to the touch and make my ass look really nice, and a t-shirt with a cool design down the back that makes me look like a tatted-up bad ass, I fix my hair perfectly, paying especial attention to the spikes and coils of hair at my temples. Every strand is in place, and now I'm sitting on the couch staring at the TV yet watching nothing, playing the waiting game.

Five o'clock brings the pair of loveless birds back to the room, and they seem in the middle of a heated debate about whether or not they're allowed to eat a certain kind of fish. Ollie gives me a breathy, "Hi," before pulling off his shirt to change for dinner. Trish slips into the bathroom. I turn up the volume on the TV so as to be spared the sound of her making a deposit in the water bank.

"We're gonna need more time," says Ollie when six o'clock draws near. "Go down, meet with your guy, and we'll join you in about twenty more minutes. That okay?"

"Sure." I give Ollie a reassuring pat on the back, then push out of the door.

To be frank, I'm kinda eager to meet with Hendry ahead of time, perhaps to give him a bit of a warning of what to expect. The glass elevator seems to move slower than usual, as if taunting me. *Ready to meet him again?* it seems to ask. *Bet you're excited. Here, let me descend even slower than I already am. Dare me to break down and trap you within me for the next three hours? I can do it. I'm a machine without feelings.*

So am I.

The doors open at the lobby, mercifully dumping me out, and I'm pleasantly surprised to find Hendry at the lobby bar. For some reason, I'd expected him to be late, not early.

I'm also a bit surprised by his attire. You'd think he was told it's a second elegant evening. He's without blazer tonight, but he's wearing a form-fitting black shirt with a striking bright silver tie. He's even wearing dress pants that hug his tight, distracting ass. His hair is tousled in the cutest way, even from behind, and I can swear the sun has somehow bleached his hair in the past few days, giving it cause to glow somehow in the dull lobby lighting. He doesn't see me at first, so I'm given the gift of getting to stare at him longingly for quite some time.

It's wonderful and awful how a craving this strong can make you abandon basic human needs. I feed off the hunger for him, emboldened by it, strengthened. I don't even feel hungry for dinner, not now.

In an instant, he flips his head around, and our eyes meet the way two stems of the same lightning bolt connect from earth to sky: in one bold, sudden, beautiful flash. Obviously I'm the earth: grounded, stubborn. Hendry's the sky: free and careless and heaven-sent.

"It isn't elegant night." It's the first thing I say before even a hello.

"Every night's an elegant night." Hendry grins, leaning back on the counter and getting a good look at me. His eyes draw up and down my frame. "You're elegant, yourself."

"Not like you." I feel underdressed next to him. It almost annoys me, if it wasn't for how sexy he looks. "I wish you'd told me that you were gonna dress up, otherwise I might've—"

"And ruin the surprise? Nah. Don't worry, Scott. Just go with the flow," he tells me.

I allow myself to sigh, attempting to calm myself down. I'm such a bundle of nerves and conflicting neurons firing around him. "I have trouble going with the flow."

"I've noticed." He turns and taps on the counter. When the bartender comes by, he says, "Hey there, Uri. Can you get me and my friend here a couple Tequila Sunrises, to help us 'go with the flow?'"

I blanch. "Before dinner?"

"You need help getting loose. The Sunrise will help." He shows the bartender his card, then smiles back at me with teeth. "You're a college boy. Don't you ever blow off steam?"

"Blow off steam? With these grades?" I chuckle nervously, bringing myself to the bar next to him and, with every fiber of my rigid unbendable body, I put on a smile and lean into a barstool. "I can't afford to do that. Hey, um ... I can totally pay you for the drink. I know how expensive this shit can be."

"It's my treat." He winks.

When the drinks arrive, I feel a sudden surge of happiness fill me before I even take the first sip. It's reminiscent of that first night Hendry and I spent together wandering the ship and getting to know one another. After a slurp, the alcohol burns the back of my throat with delight, and its taste is sweet and sharp. Without my permission, a smile pastes itself across my dumb face.

"Good things happen when you let go a bit," says Hendry, and I try not to hear that in the voice of the guy from my dreams.

"Scary things happen too," I return.

"Better to see the scary and fear it at least once or twice in your life than to not have seen it at all and rob yourself of the pleasure." He sips his glass like a prince, delicate and regal and deliberate, his every movement.

"I feel like I'm afraid every day of my life. Fear's where I live," I confess. Just one sip of alcohol and I'm already feeling a looseness consume me, a looseness I cannot fight. "Who would I be without it? I'm terrified to find out. Maybe it's why I don't drink. I'm terrified to know what's underneath all the years of care and thought and ... *plans*." I sip. It burns. I smile and dare myself to sip again, then again.

"Only one way to find out." Hendry's face tightens, and he faces me with his button nose scrunched in thought. "We transform without fear. Scott, dude, I'm telling you, when I was growing up, I was so scared of everything. My brother taught me so much about ... fear. We don't know fucking anything over here in our big safe houses and our cushy offices and our lame schools. We don't know fuck-all about fear."

Leaning into the counter, my arm presses into his. His eyes meet mine. I cradle my Tequila Sunrise and sip again as our eyes glue together and I think all about fear.

"I'm afraid I'm a repressed alcoholic," I confess.

"I'm afraid I'm a repressed homo. Don't tell my buddies," he adds in a whisper.

I laugh. I laugh a bit too much. "Oh, you."

Hendry shrugs cutely, his tie bobbing. "Y'know, I think I get you. I respect and admire your loyalty. You're mega-committed to your future. That's serious integrity."

I smile, taken a bit by the compliment. "I have it all planned out to the end," I admit, thinking of all the hours and credits still waiting for me to complete them. "It's just a bit ... daunting, the road I've paved ahead of myself. It's uphill, for years to come, winding up a mountain of homework and student loans and ... and night sweats."

He sees the agony in my eyes. "Though I respect your undying commitment," he says tentatively, "don't you think, like, you also owe it to yourself to kinda ... *enjoy* the journey, too? It doesn't all have to be suffering and paperwork."

"I *do* enjoy it," I say, then stare into my drink and wonder who I'm trying to convince. This is the life I wanted, right?

"You have really honest eyes," he tells me.

I push a hand into my cheek and slump against the counter, batting my eyes. "Oh, these old things?"

"I feel really secure around you, Scott." He finishes his drink, then pushes the emptied cup across the counter. "We should keep this going between us. Whatever this is. Do you feel it?"

It's weird how just a number of words correctly arranged in a sentence can sober you the fuck up. I straighten my back and lift my brows, caught by surprise. "This? Feel this? Yes, I feel—I feel things."

"Me too." The smile on his face disappears and, in its stead, a look of hunger fills his eyes and a tightness twists his lips. What's this pretty guy thinking about?

That's when Ollie and Trish appear out of thin fucking air to wreck our moment.

"Hey there!" says Hendry, the cheeriness returning to his face. "You must be Ollie, the best friend and confidant. And you must be Trish, the beautiful girlfriend."

Trish looks amused, though it seems more mocking in my eyes than genuine. "Yep!" says Ollie brightly. "You're Henry. Sorry, Hen*dry*. The mystery man Scott's told us about."

You know that feeling when you drink too much alcohol, and your butthole gets so relaxed you think you could shit your pants?

"We can solve some of that mystery over a tasty dinner," Hendry suggests.

The suggestion is taken in an instant, a ravenous hunger possessing the odd quartet of us. A pair of two-person tables slide together for us, and I end up sitting right across from Hendry, which puts Ollie at my left side and Trish next to Hendry. The work of ordering is dealt with in time, as Trish has questions about each of the courses and nothing seems to be acceptable without twelve modifications. Ollie, naturally, orders the same thing as her.

"What do you do?" asks Ollie.

"I'm undecided at the moment," Hendry admits. "I've had some recent changes in my life and attending college has, regrettably, been a thing I've had to postpone. I'm staying with some of my buddies in the Woodlands."

"Oh, so you're from here?" asks Ollie.

"If by 'here' you mean Texas, then yes. North of Houston. Are you guys from Texas as well?"

North of Houston? *We're* from Houston. Except I've been stolen by Austin. "They're in Houston. I'm in Austin," I answer, stunned.

"Just a couple hours away." Hendry seems to find this information satisfying, smiling in its discovery. I find it a bit burdening, as hours to me sounds like a lot of commuting if we plan to continue knowing one another after the ship returns to port.

"Recent life changes, you said?" asks Ollie.

"Yes, but I'll save that for another time, if you don't mind. None of you want to hear my sob story, not over a light dinner. Let's discuss cheery things," states Hendry. "Tell me about how you and the lovely Trish met."

Trish gives him a sidelong glance, and I daresay it looks almost flattered.

Ollie launches into the whole story, which involves a class senior year of high school and a bad grade, which resulted in the pair of them studying over books under a specific tree by the science building. He recalls it like it was yesterday. The sun was shining. Birds sang in the branches. Blah, blah.

"Hey," I interrupt when Ollie mentions something about recruiters on campus. "Tell them about your brother, Hendry." I face the others. "He has a brother in the Army. His brother taught him everything he knows. What's his name? I didn't ask."

A pensive expression takes Hendry quite suddenly. Then, after a strangely long second of hesitation, he answers, "Josiah."

"Army," says Trish just as the server shows up to lay a salad in front of her. "Did he fight in Iraq? Older brother or younger?"

Oh, listen to her acting all interested. I roll my eyes and chug the last of my Sunrise.

"Older," answers Hendry. "And yes. He did ... until he was injured. He's home now."

Trish is genuinely taken aback, her eyes turning into two glass orbs. Just then, the server shows up to set salads in front of us, then tells us to enjoy our meal.

It's Ollie who speaks next. "I'm sorry to hear that, man. Thanks to your brother for his service."

"Much appreciated," says Hendry, putting a smile on his face, perhaps in a sad attempt to keep the mood light. "The war changed him quite a bit, and the therapy was hard, but he's the strongest dude I know. I'm proud of him." Suddenly, he lifts his glass of tea. "Let's make a toast. To cool new friends and adventures. May we never, ever know what's coming. May life always be a great big fun-loving surprise full of ... joy and fulfillment."

"To joy and fulfillment," says Ollie, lifting his water.

"Joy," agrees Trish lamely, lifting hers.

I lift my own, the shock unable to clear from my face. Hendry meets my eyes and, with a shrug and a smile, he taps our glasses with his own and brings the beverage to his lips. We sip in a gentle silence.

Then, Hendry grins and says, "Thanks so much for letting me join you guys. For real. I love the buds I came with, sure, but I'm really enjoying making some new, kick-ass friends. Hey, I happened to overhear some of your dietary concerns when you ordered. Are you gonna eat those evil body-hating croutons, or can I steal them off your salad?"

"Go to town," says Trish, turning up her nose while Hendry pokes his fork at them.

The rest of the dinner takes a light turn, and I never recover from the spinning of the Tequila Sunrise. I laugh harder than I ought to at every joke, and when Ollie starts to tell a story about a dumb thing he did in high school once, I chime in with my own version of the tale. I don't care how loud my voice is.

Let the world know I'm alive. Let them see me living. Let every passenger on this fucking boat pay witness to my overflowing joy.

After enjoying dinner, the four of us carry the conversation through the boat, past the casino, and to the theater where a magic show is about to begin. We get four seats very close to the stage, remarkably. There are tiny tables spaced evenly along the aisle for drinks because, well, alcohol is any cruise line's bread and butter. Trish and Ollie share one while Hendry and I share another, and before the show even begins, I've already downed two more drinks. When the server comes by for a third time to check on whether Trish or Ollie would like anything, I tell the short man from Bulgaria that I'd like a pair of Tequila Sunrises for Hendry and I. Hendry throws an arm over the back of my chair, smiling.

Just the touch of his fingers grazing my opposite shoulder sets me afire. I know his arm is right behind me. I want to lean into him, fall into his arms, yet still I don't quite feel allowed to do that yet, even as tipsy as I am. I want to savor every moment with him. I turn to face him just as the lights dim, and catch a pretty sight of Hendry marveling at the stage as it fills up with lights. I don't need to see the stage; I watch the colors glitter in his eyes and his lips part with awe.

When there's another alcoholic beverage in my hand, I drink half of it in the space of five minutes and watch the show. The good thing about sitting up-close in a magic show is that you see everything. The bad thing about sitting up-close in a magic show ...

... is that you see everything.

"The fuck?" I shout out, startling Hendry. "You pulled the scarf out of your pocket!"

Despite the room being inundated by big dramatic music over the sound system, the magician heard me. I see it in his eyes. Still, he continues his act, and I'm left to watch in annoyance as the caped fool wriggles a long "magic rod" out of a short hat that rests on a table with one leg in the middle. Obviously he's pulling the stupid rod out of the leg of the table, which must be hollow. He lifts the rod into the air, presenting it, and he gives his showiest white-toothed grin to the crowd, who applaud stupidly.

I take another gulp, lean forward, then shout, "We see right through you, idiot!"

"*Scott!*" whispers Ollie, hushing me.

I laugh. This isn't a magic show. This is a comedy. Can't anyone else see that? I look around to gather other likeminded witnesses, but they're all entranced by the magician, caught in his spell.

I jab Hendry in the ribs with my elbow. "You're seeing this too, right?"

Hendry turns to look at me, and the humor is in his eyes as well, but he doesn't respond. He just looks at me smilingly.

"Yeah," I say, taking his smile to be the answer I was looking for. "So dumb. I want to be fooled. Isn't that the point of magic? I don't want to see everything. I don't want to know the secrets. I want to be *fooled*."

"Shut up," says a dude from behind.

I turn and glare balefully at him. "You want to say that to my face instead of the back of my ..." I feel a hiccup coming. It doesn't come. I resume. "... the back of my head?"

The dude is maybe forty-something. He has a dirty mustache, bumpy skin, and crow's feet. "I'm trying to watch the damn show."

"You *are* watching the show," I spit back. "You're watching the behind-the-scenes too, this close up. It's a goddamn instructional video. Learning How To *Magic*: A Guide."

Hendry laughs, watching me go at it with this guy. I know I'm not myself. I know that I am a bit—maybe a lot—loosened by the drinks I've put into me. But I don't care. Twenty-one years of repressed anger and vexation paint my eyes red quite suddenly, and this dude behind me has magically become the reason that I've been so controlling and miserable. He's the reason I micromanage and drive people insane. He's the reason I'm single.

"Get out of my face," says the man.

"Stay tuned, and you'll learn how to bend over and pull a bunny out of your ass," I go on. Hendry guffaws at that. At least one audience member in my one-man show is laughing.

At once, I'm on my back, and the man with the mustache is on top of me. I put up my hands and scream as the man tries to make at my face in a fit of fury. The hilarious part is, amidst all the screaming and violence, all I hear is the magician's stupid fucking music.

The next moment, Hendry's shouting at the man. I twist my neck and catch a glimpse of Ollie and Trish, both of them staring at me with horror in their eyes.

I don't even know what just happened.

Freed from the man, I'm on my feet and charging after him. I have no idea what I'm doing. Hendry shouts out. The magician's music hits a crescendo, and I've toppled the man. Now it's my turn to be on top.

"*Abracadabra, mother fucker!!*"

Hands move to hug me from behind. *Mmm, lovers' hands.* When I turn to get a peek,

I realize it's the security officers who are pulling me off the guy.

"He started it!" I scream. "It's *his* fucking magic show!" I point at the magician who, even with all the commotion in the front row that draws the attention of half his audience, is still performing. *HE IS STILL FUCKING PERFORMING.* "Stop! Get the fuck off me!"

My eyes connect with Hendry. He stands next to my friends and all the joy and all the laughter has left his eyes.

Maybe it's the sight of him that sobers me, despite my head still spinning. The security guards drag me away. I keep twisting my head to watch, looking on as another officer helps the mustached man to his feet, looking on as Ollie and Trish argue with the officer about something I won't know because I can't hear them. All I hear as I'm pulled away is the magician's mounting, thrumming music as he spreads a proud hand, sweeps his cape, and makes another thing disappear.

Cue the applause.

[The Lost Art of Giving A Fuck]

Something I've learned tonight: the cruise ship has this adorable little cruise ship jail onboard, and at times it can act like a drunk tank where they take the disorderly. I never in a hundred years would have pictured myself as one of the drunken fools who would be thrown into such a contraption.

And the room they put you in is nothing kind to the eyes. It's plain. There's nothing in it. And while you're stuck in those four walls, all you do is hate yourself, reflect on every one of your stupid, drunken actions, and cry.

Mostly cry.

"You don't seem like the type of fellow we toss in here," I remember the officer telling me. He said a lot of things to me. The dude with the mustache isn't pressing charges. Apparently his wife saw *him* as the aggressor. Also, my friends seemed to back up that point of view, citing the man as the one who threw the first bitch-slap. I don't care. I instigated it. Soon after, my head cleared just a little bit and I broke down and cried and kept repeating some dumb phrase over and over, something like: *I don't know what happened, I don't know what happened, I don't know what happened ...*

I slipped in a big ol' puddle, that's what happened. Now, regretfully, the only reason I'm wet is because of my own tears.

Considering it's past midnight, and despite their usual policies, some authority figure with pretty red hair whose name I already forgot allows me back to my room, but with the assurance and promise that I stay there, rest for the night, then try to enjoy my day in Cozumel tomorrow. I looked up at the kind woman, my breath reeking of the cocktail of worry and regret in my belly, and said, "Can I have my ID card back?" She gave it a glance, handed it to me and said, "Happy twenty-second birthday, Mr. Berringer."

When I return to the room, Ollie's in the shower and Trish is propped up on the bed watching TV. At my arrival, she turns her stony face to me.

"I don't want to hear it. Not a word," I mutter miserably, shutting the cabin door and slumping on the couch-bed, not bothering to change or look at my frightfully disturbed self in the mirror.

Trish continues to watch me. I feel her intense staring on the side of my face.

I can't stand it. I close my eyes. I was sure I didn't have any more tears in me after all the crying I did in that tiny scary room, but a whole new wave of awesome decides to invade my eyes and make a war down my face. I hear all the tinking and tapping of spears and shields and swords as the tears fall.

I sniffle once, miserably. "What's the point anyway?" I ask no one in particular. "Two more days and we're back home. Two more days and whatever this thing is between me and that *guy* I haven't even kissed yet or done fucking anything with is *over*. If it isn't already. I fucked everything up."

"I like him."

I wipe my eyes and turn to her.

Trish shrugs, entirely unaffected by my insistence on snotting all over myself. Her Malibu Barbie hair bounces when she shrugs. "I do," she says simply. "I think he's kind. I think he's gentle. I think ... well, especially after hearing what he said when you were taken away, I think—"

"What'd he say?" I ask.

She rolls her eyes, then twists her body around to face me. "If you'd let me *finish*, Scott. I was going to say, he thinks the whole thing was *his* fault because he was the one who said you needed to loosen up, and he went and bought you that first drink that started it all."

That hurts somehow. "It wasn't his fault. None of this was his fault."

"I can't believe you jumped on that man who was twice your size and could've beaten you into a pancake." Trish cackles once, shakes her head, then says, "You got some balls, Scott. '*Abracadabra, mother fucker!*' Wow. You're a crazy bitch."

I stare at her for a moment, unsure how to take her words. When our eyes meet, a weird stab of humor tickles us, and suddenly we start to laugh. I laugh twice as hard as she does, likely because a platoon of little tear soldiers is still trying to push out of my eyes.

"Hey, Scott," she says when I recover. "If I ever need to set Ollie straight on anything, I'm gonna sic your crazy ass on him."

I picture that last sight of Hendry's totally humorless face in the theater. "What do I do?" I ask, the laughs spent, at a loss.

"What the fuck do you think?" She smirks at me, as though I'm an idiot. "Go have your night and a half with him. He'll be happy to hear you haven't been quarantined for the rest of the trip. They do that, you know. You could've been locked up in cruise jail and arrested when we get to Galveston."

"But I'm confined to the room. It was sort of ... It was sort of the agreement I made with the officer or whoever. Rest and cool down here and wake up and have a day in Cozumel."

"Ooh. And we should follow the rules like good boys and girls." Trish points the remote and mashes a button. "These channels suck."

I look at my hands. "That mustached guy totally didn't deserve my douchebaggery."

"The magician was tragic," says Trish, sneering. "You could see when he hid shit in his jacket."

I smile at her and try to have a moment of meaningfulness. "You saw it, too. Thanks."

She snorts. "Go get your Harris boy, you annoying twat. You can thank me later."

"His name's Hendry, bitch, but thanks for the sentiment." I wink at her. She rolls her eyes irritably, despite a smile teasing out of the corner of her cherry lips.

Ollie is still showering when I leave the room. I make my way to the glass elevators, curious where the hell Hendry might be. For all I know, he's made his way back to his room and fallen asleep, his night destroyed by my dumb, drunken shenanigans.

When the elevator empties me up onto the lido, I spot a security guard standing at the bar. He doesn't see me. Feeling like some fugitive, I calmly stroll the opposite edge of the lido, ascending the stairs to the panorama deck with my pulse dancing in my neck. Gosh, I feel so subversive. I'm a robber dashing out of sight of the police. My stolen treasure of choice is a good time.

It's strange yet oddly expected that I find him in the first place I look.

Hendry's still fixed up as he was for the evening, shirt tucked in his fitted dress pants.

His tie hangs loose, and the shirt's unbuttoned a few. He stares into the darkness, his hair, a mess of blond waves dancing on his forehead, to match the crashing of watery ones below.

I don't make it halfway to him before he notices me, spinning and lifting his brows in surprise. "You're okay!" he exclaims.

I study him, suspicious of his cheeriness. "I totally ruined the night," I say, as if a kind reminder.

"Yeah, you did." He smiles. "Totally made a muck of it all."

I put my shameful self in front of him. "I think it goes without saying, I sorta pictured tonight going rather ... differently."

"Yeah?"

"I pictured us all hanging out. I pictured them going off and doing their thing and ..." I sigh. There's two days left of the cruise. What have I to lose? "And I thought ... maybe I'd get to know you even better. I ..." I swallow hard. There's not much alcohol left in me to chill my stupid nerves. "I ... I like you."

"I like you too, Scott."

Now we're two clueless dumb boys in high school trading verbal love notes and blushing and twirling our hair. Listen to us.

"You want to get to know me better?" he asks me, taking a step forward. I smell his cologne. Maybe it's his deodorant. Or maybe it's just his natural, perfect, clean smell.

"Yes."

He takes another step. "What about me?"

I take a step back. He's moving into my bubble. I feel my heart racing. "Everything."

"What, specifically?"

He's tossed the bait. I'm the stubborn fish, fickle and slippery. "I want to get to know ..." He gets so close, I feel his breath on my face. Or maybe it's a stray breeze. "I want to get better acquainted with ..." I feel his heat. Or it's my heat. Maybe he's the big fish and I'm throwing the hook. I'm throwing the hook and waiting for him to pull. "With ..."

"With what?"

"Your lips."

Hendry anticipated my move, swims up to me, and bites. The assault of intimacy, his face pressing into mine, rends my nerves to shreds of human yarn. His lips are warm and full and wet, pressed against my thick and dry ones. His tongue teases out, like an experiment. I embrace it, opening my mouth to him and letting all of him in.

It might be an odd thing to observe, but my very first thought when his tongue enters is: *he has good breath, he tastes so good, his smell draws me in.*

As fast as it began, it's over. He pulls away and his eyes flash. "It's your birthday," he says, remembering.

Fuck. His memory. His good memory. I find that so, so fucking hot. "Twenty-two never felt so like twenty-one," I remark.

"Wanna ... celebrate?" His eyes bleed with thirst. "Maybe you'd like to ... get to know one another a little better ... elsewhere?"

My eyes flash. "Where?"

"A cabin on the seventh deck."

He hardly gets the words out before we're rushing down a pair of stairs and past a security guard who, though he looks up, does not seem to recognize me. Really, I'm quite sure everyone's forgotten about the whole thing by now. I sure as fuck have.

And I forget about the whole rest of the world too when Hendry opens the door to a small cabin on the seventh—an interior cabin without a balcony or windows—and he pulls shut the door so hard, its slam rattles the wall.

"Take off all my clothes," Hendry orders me with a sexy, lopsided smirk. "Get to know me better."

"Not so fast." Almost gently, I pull him to the center of the room. "I want to ... know what I'm getting into."

"Oh?"

"I want to ... take time unwrapping my birthday present."

Then, slow as a snake, I circle Hendry as he stands there and lets me. I circle him and observe every inch of that shirt, clinging to his sexy body. Behind him, I run my eyes down to his tight ass. I don't dare touch it yet, my insides exploding with anticipation. I come to the front and take hold of his loosened tie.

Our eyes meet. "Acquainted?" he asks.

I tug on the tie. He lurches forward, and his dimples pop out when he grins hungrily. Using the tie like a leash, I bring his face back to mine. "Not yet," I whisper.

Then the tie comes off. One at a time, I slowly unbutton his shirt. Pop, one button. Pop, two buttons. I unwrap my gift with the excruciating slowness of a person who cares to preserve his wrapping paper. When they're all undone, I gently spread the shirt apart.

My, oh my. Those smooth, sexy pecs, resting atop a cage of subtle abs. They're not overwhelming and chiseled, like a bodybuilder or a fitness model. These are the muscles of the adorable boy next door that you've had a crush on your whole life. You peel off his wrapping paper one bit at a time, and for each piece, you're closer to his true essence. He becomes vulnerable. He becomes open. His secrets are set before your eyes, and there is nothing sexier than that kind of intimacy.

The shirt slips off, and it's just a sexy man named Hendry in a pair of tight fitted dress pants and a shiny leather belt. Above that, the tanned perfection of this smooth, silky dream boy. He watches me do all this. He smirks, a glint of power in his eyes.

Yeah, even when I think I'm in control, it's really Hendry who's got me gripped.

Even his nipples watch me. I can't hold back any more, not with all of this laid out before me. I latch my mouth to his chest, wetting a path of kisses to his nipple. His breathing quickens. I suck and twist on his nipple, my tongue playing games and seeing what other noises I can earn from him.

His breath goes jagged. He moans. Then, his hands take hold of my body. The act of his arms coming forward makes his pecs flex out, and suddenly his nipple is hard as stone.

I bite.

"Oh, god ... Fuck, Scott. Fuuuck."

My hands run down his backside, slowly, gently, and then they become two ravenous, greedy animals when they reach his tight ass. I grab a firm hold of it, breathing into his chest deeply. Then, just as sudden, I detach from his nipple and thrust my hips into his, where I make another discovery. Both our cocks are hard. Throbbing, even. Just with that thrust of my hip, I feel his cock flex against me.

And then: "I want you to tie me up."

Hendry comes out of the trance and stares at me. Then, amusement crosses his face. "Yeah? Really?"

"It's a fantasy of mine. It's ... It's a thing I've always wanted to ... to ..."

"You need to let go of control, huh?" He grins smartly. "Let some big bad boy like me be the boss, huh?"

"I need it so bad."

"Drank so much, lost your head, nearly took off someone else's, and you're still too much in control, huh?" It's Hendry's turn to circle around me. "Have you become well-acquainted with me, yet?"

He takes my hands, then gently pulls them to my back.

"H-Hendry ..."

I feel the silk kiss of his tie as it wraps around my wrists, softly at first, but second by the second, they grow tighter and tighter until all movement or use of my hands is seized at once. The way he makes me his, it's so easy. There's no loud words. No forcing. Just ...

Just the dance of words and smooth skin. "You're not getting out of these binds anytime soon, bro."

"No," I agree, breathing hard. "I-I'm not."

He comes around to my front, and his face is sultry, wicked, and handsome. I'm so turned on that I'm leaking in my pants, and there's no way I can hide it.

He notices too. He gives my cock a flick, and I flinch away, wincing. That makes him laugh. "You look mighty restrained in those pants. Must be *crammed* inside there."

I try to act cool. I play tough. Is this the real me coming out, or another of my control-game schemes? "Yeah? What're you gonna do about it?"

"Hey, nice shirt."

The compliment totally throws me off. "Uh, thanks. It's nothing, really, just a—"

He grabs the neck of the shirt and jerks, his arms flexing beautifully as it tears halfway down my torso, opening me up.

"Dude!" I cry out in protest. "My shirt!"

But in the next instant, his mouth attaches to mine, and I'm snapped right back into the realm of looseness and sexiness and freedom. In one instant, the ripping of the shirt changes from a moment of grief to one of the sexiest things that's ever happened to me. *He fucking tore me out of my clothes.* Suddenly, I crave him tearing me out of a hundred of my shirts.

While he kisses me, his sneaky hands unbutton my pants and work them down my legs. I feel his warm hands running along my hips, and when those mighty fingers grab hold of my underwear, I anticipate hungrily the release of my totally boned-up and pent-up toy. He pulls once, and the mere freedom of my cock as it points into the air is enough to make me breathe sweet mercy on his face.

The next instant finds my face pressed to the bed, and he spreads my legs apart with his own. "Fuck, fuck, fuck," I breathe, my hard cock smashed against the bed under me. The sheets are so soft, it's like a hand cradles my horned-up junk. Every time I shift my hips, it's like I'm jerking off. I squirm into the bed.

"Fuck. Exactly," Hendry agrees as I hear the tear of a wrapper.

From the sound of that condom wrapper and whatever else he's hiding behind me, I feel like the decision's already been made. Maybe I made it when I begged to get tied up, begged to let him have control, begged for a freedom I could never grant myself.

He leans over, all his weight pressing into my back and my still-bound hands, and he whispers into my ear: "You're gonna know more about me than any of my best buddies." I feel a slippery finger tease into my crack, sending a wave of joy through me. I feel so vulnerable. I feel so open. Can't hide a thing. Don't want to. "You're gonna get to know me so well, Scott."

His voice carries all the humor of our conversation on the deck, but it's so serious now. It's going to happen. I'm going to feel him inside me. It occurs to me that, in truth, I'm *still* in control. I could tell him to stop at any time, but ...

"Let go," he breathes into my ear, just as the head of his cock touches my hole.

I don't want him to stop. I don't want to know I have control. I want to be fooled.

"Oh god."

"Scott," he breathes, biting my ear.

I shiver as I open up, feeling him slide deeper inside. I'm so horny and repressed that I'm already close. This is going to be very difficult for me, lasting long enough so as not to embarrass myself. I never thought I'd be the guy who could get off while being penetrated. I am someone else on this ship.

Or this is the real me. The real me, freed from a cage of my own making.

He pushes in and out, pumping me slowly yet forcefully. I can't do a thing but breathe and snort into the bed sheets. Each thrust he gives of his powerful hips, I feel a ridiculously pleasurable stroke of my own cock. I can't stop him. I can't control it. If I get too close, I'm going to cum whether I want to yet or not.

He really *is* in control.

"Hendry. Oh, fuck. I'm so close already."

"You're not cumming until I let you cum," he says to my back, then grips my hair and pulls as he rides me.

My cock is a second away from exploding all over his clean sheets, but Hendry's rhythm and his grip on my hair and the sound of our jagged breaths makes that second last forever.

Only when you've let go of everything, can you keep hold of anything.

"I can't hold it," I moan desperately.

"Me neither. Fuck it," he says back, an adorably out-of-character confession. "Let go."

Without my hands, I feel my insides harden and my balls tighten as I squeeze a mess of cum between the sheets and my belly, exploding white-hot and wet, and the shout that issues from my throat is animal. Hendry's grip on my hair gives me a moment of alarm as he pulls, jerks back, and dumps all his cum while still fucking me. His orgasm goes on for ages; wave after wave, pulse after pulse, until his grip loosens and he collapses onto me.

Breathing heavy, the pair of us just lie there, utterly spent and drifting in a sea of bliss. Neither of us move and, to be frank, I doubt either of us wishes to. Even with my hands still bound, he lies there on top of me with his arms cradling my face, listening as our breath and our hearts slowly calm down.

"I like you a lot," he whispers into my ear. "Let me keep you."

"Considering you still got me tied up," I point out, "I guess I'm all yours."

"I wanna put you in my pocket and take you home with me."

"If only."

It's a matter of minutes later that he gently undoes the tie at my back and, without a care for the mess we've made, we curl up right where we are, mostly naked, and say goodnight, neither of us having the strength to mention that only two days remain before we are sent back into our respective cages.

[A Mess Of Us]

The morning finds me with an unshakable expression on my face. And it's not just the wetness left there by Hendry's kisses.

It's like discovering a brand new flavor of ice cream in my freezer. A new flavor I didn't know exists. A flavor that sits on my tongue.

An option.

The sound of the shower stirs me from the peace I was having. He left the door open, which I take for an invitation. Slipping out of my torn, cum-stained shirt, I push into the bathroom. A naked Hendry turns, a lathering of shampoo already in his hair, and he grins knowingly. The shower is cramped as fuck with one person alone, so I figure why not, and squeeze in to make it even more so. At one point, his elbow knocks the knob, turning the water ice cold for an instant. He shrieks and suffers the onslaught of chilliness for the both of us for six full seconds before managing to twist the knob back to warm.

He lets me borrow a shirt of his, since he decimated my old one, and I find it to be quite fitting and soft. Already, we're sharing clothes like a pair of college buddies. "Keep it," he tells me. "A memento."

"More like, you owe me a fucking shirt," I tease back, my old one finding the trash bin.

For an hour after our shower, we sit on the bed and do nothing at all but watch TV. With no windows in the room, the world feels eerily timeless. It could be morning, noon, or night; neither of us would know.

"Got any plans for Cozumel?" I ask.

"None at all. You?"

"Thinking I'll pick up a bottle of authentic Mexican vanilla for my mom," I say. "And maybe a bottle of Kahlúa. When she heard Ollie and I were taking this trip, she begged me to snatch some for her."

"Yeah?"

"If I don't, I'm pretty sure she'll beat me up at Thanksgiving." My arm is thrown over Hendry's back, and he's nuzzled into me, cuddling and still sleepy-eyed.

"Wish my family did things like that."

"Like what?"

"Thanksgiving things. Holiday things." Hendry's hand plays up and down my chest, tickling my nipple when it passes each time. "Is it too soon to say I think your mom sounds cool as fuck?"

"Too soon? I wouldn't know. Is there a rulebook or some shit?"

"I'm gonna miss you."

I bring my hand to his hair, twirling my fingers in it. Time is strange on a cruise ship. Letting go of your daily expectations takes no time at all, and even just after four days, you feel like you've been here a month. Whatever this is between Hendry and I, it in no way feels like something that just began five days ago in a boarding pass line. My feelings are pulled apart into a hundred pieces and they're scattered fucking everywhere. I have no idea how to put all of this back together.

"We still have two whole days," he points out, trying to cheer himself up. "Why am I worrying about this so much?"

"For real. That's *my* job."

"Can we do the Cozumel thing together? I wanna get that cool vanilla for your mom."

"What about your buddies? Do you have any excursions or ... plans with them?"

"Not really." Hendry shrugs. "I'm feeling a lot of distance with them lately. They're all talking about what they're gonna do in the fall and none of it includes me anymore."

"What do you mean?"

"College. I ... I had to drop out because of my life and ..." Hendry sighs into my chest, then rolls to his side and props up his head, facing me. His feet dangle off the bed. "Things changed really fast when my brother came home injured. My parents split just before it happened. Mom went into this depression thing. Whole family's wrecked, man."

"I'm so sorry, Hendry."

"Me too. Needless to say, money situation is drastically changed. Despite my mom's insistence not to worry about her, and that I should go off to make something of myself ... I can't for a handful of reasons. Namely, tuition isn't easy. I have no way to commute. The cost of a dorm or apartment is just ridiculous."

I let his words stew, thinking on them long and hard. In the very next instant, he seems to dismiss his own worries and tells me some funny story about two of his buddies and an "almost homo moment" they had involving a life guard and a poolside prank and one too many beers garnished with orange slices. I run my hand through his hair, listening, but my mind won't stop working.

Options. Choices. Life. Living.

Dreams. That thing called happy.

Letting go.

"Why does it feel like I've known you for, like, ever?" he asks rhetorically, then laughs. "I'm telling you all this stuff and, like ..."

Letting go of fear. "I like you too, Hendry. This was meant to happen. That little puddle of H_2O by the pool sent me diving for you like an oasis to a dying man in the desert."

"Am I the oasis?" he asks cutely.

I nod.

"So ... I make you wet?"

I smack him hard on the shoulder. "Don't cheapen this deep moment I'm trying to have with you, punk!"

He rubs his shoulder, laughing, then says, "Sorry, bromo. In all fairness, I have this gut feeling you and I are gonna share a lot more deep moments."

"I like your gut feeling."

We lose even more of our morning to the distraction of two mouths ... *and a lot of wet.*

Since Trish knew damn well where I was headed last night—as she basically sent me after Hendry—I figure it unnecessary to check in with them, and tell myself they could use a day together in Cozumel without me.

Then, as ever-playful fate would have it, when Hendry and I make it to the lido deck to grab some breakfast, we find Trish and Ollie sitting by the window. After filling two plates with food from the buffet, Hendry leads us right to their table and helps himself to a seat, greeting my friends cheerfully.

While Trish and Hendry talk about every little thing they know about Cozumel, Ollie gives me that knowing look across the table. I have to look away to avoid my face flushing, because I'm pretty sure Ollie's thinking: *You got some last night, didn't ya? Wink, wink.*

Then he says: "Gonna grab some more fruit. Anyone need anything?"

"I'll come with you. I forgot utensils," says Hendry with a chuckle. "Be back." He gives me a wink, then marches off with Ollie.

Trish and I are left in a peculiar staring contest. Her eyes flit down to my plate of scrambled eggs, bacon, toast, and everything else evil under the sun that she and Ollie are not allowed to have. I lift my cup of orange juice to my lips and take a sip. She watches.

"Tasty," I let her know cruelly. Then, she swipes the cup from my hand in one quick-as-a-ninja movement and takes a swig. I gawp. "B-But your ... your cleanse!"

"Fuck the cleanse!" she cries, desperately gulping the rest. "I'm fucking starved! You gonna finish that bacon?" She asks this of the bacon strips I haven't even touched yet, then helps herself without my answer, stealing half of them. After a moment of watching her in awe, she notices and sneers at me, gnashing her teeth. "Don't tell Ollie. The cleanse is good for him. Bitch needs discipline."

I smile. "Don't we all."

"As if I don't know he's *snuck* things this whole trip. I'm dying here." She eats.

And eats and eats and eats.

I turn and watch Ollie and Hendry in the breakfast line talking, distracting themselves from their task of utensils and food with conversation, then bursting into laughter. Their connection makes me smile.

That thought that rested on my tongue like a brand new ice cream flavor this morning sends a fire of inspiration through my gut.

Our time in Cozumel is the best of all the ports and it is the simplest. We stroll from kiosk to kiosk, crowded store to crowded store. We get five shirts for twenty bucks. He gets my mom's vanilla. I get the Kahlúa from an eager man in a store. I buy him a wrestler's mask too and we laugh when he puts it on and growls, poised to pounce me.

Back on the ship and after a delicious dinner settles in our bellies, Hendry gives us a lesson at the casino. "It's about the roll," he tells us at the craps table. "Face your lucky numbers up—mine are double six—and then you stare Lady Luck in the face, and ..."

He pitches the dice.

He loses.

The laughter we've experienced together tonight, even Ollie and Trish included, is enough to make up for any losses I've had this whole trip. I've made out with the greatest gain, if you ask me.

For the final two nights, there's a hired comedian onboard. We sit in the mess of a crowded audience and listen to a man dressed like a cowboy as he tells his best southern and redneck humor. I guess it makes sense, being on a ship that comes out of Galveston. He knows his crowd. It's a funny thing, comedy. It's like magic without the sweep of a cape and the sleight of hand, only his arsenal of tricks is in fearlessness, relatable stories, and timing.

I stay in Hendry's room again, retiring that fucking couch-bed in Ollie's room for good. Of course, I made a trip for some clothes and necessary toiletries. I think Ollie and Trish could use the alone time in the bedroom, not that I want to picture what bat-shit crazy stuff goes on behind *their* closed doors. I'm pretty sure it involves black leather and Trish bearing a cat o' nine tails—maybe even ten.

"I can't wait to be lazy as fuck with you tomorrow," says Hendry between bouts of feverishly making out in the bed—which has had a merciful changing of sheets since we so indelicately wrecked them. "I can't stand that we only have one more day."

"When you're happy in life," I put back to him, "dude, the vacation never ends."

He punches my lips with his own, giving a little bite before letting them go. "Here's to never letting the vacation end."

When we kiss, I realize I've never felt so alive. And I've never felt so afraid. I've been quiet and careful and scared to stir up a calm pool of water, all these years. Now, a beast is awakened. I want to shout and dominate and claim what's mine. I want to shatter the waters. I want to be happy.

I want to be brazen.

[To Be Brazen]

"Does it make me an annoying optimist for believing Schrödinger's cat is alive?" I ask as we play the mini-golf course on the highest deck, which is being pummeled by wind.

Hendry scrunches up his face, his nose wrinkling adorably. "Dinger Who??"

"Don't hit your golf ball too hard," I warn him. "With this wind, it'll land in fucking Australia."

He aims for the hole, squints with strict calculation, then taps the ball. It goes five times farther than intended. I try not to laugh.

"Maybe we should've heeded the warning sign at the beginning of the course," says Hendry with a scoff. "Winds are really high today. Clouds rolling in."

"Funny you say that." I give my ball a tap. It goes way the fuck *that* way and not enough *this* way. "The reason we met was because I ignored a warning sign."

Hendry meets my eyes. "That's right. You told me. Deck is slippery when—"

I drop my club and push him to the railing, the wind throwing his hair in every direction. "So fuck the warnings." I kiss him furiously, my hand gripping the back of his neck and my lips never letting up. He breathes into me, uneven, taken by surprise. I like this change in me.

I like surprising him.

When we pull apart, we discover a mother unsuccessfully shielding her kid's eyes from the sight of us. We look at each other and bust out laughing.

The whole last day is full of laughs.

It's a day at sea. No ports. We're heading home to Galveston, arrival time six-something in the dark of a morning we have all been secretly dreading. For a very specific reason that I will not yet divulge, I am elated and feel little of the dread anymore.

Fear can be your friend, too. It isn't just an imaginary ghost you see in the dark. It isn't just the bear that's happened on your tent. It isn't just the robber at gunpoint or the fire alarm going off or a really scary dream. Fear is also the pulse-pumping moment before you kiss someone for the first time. Fear is also the feeling you get while the tiny marble bounces around the roulette table before settling on your number. Fear is the moment before an actor steps onstage to give the greatest performance of their lifetime.

I am filled with a prickly, unsettling fear, and it makes me smile because it gives me a strange, unknowing strength. Hendry must see it because he seems inspired by it. I don't catch him in a single moment of sadness.

The final sunset of our cruise finds us—all four of us—on the lido deck eating pizza (Trish gave up her cover), giving a shit about nothing, and watching a superhero movie on the big screen, its glow painting our faces in shades of blue and white and flashing red. Trish, who I'll assume was abducted by gulf-loitering aliens and replaced with a totally different individual the night I went berserk on a poor mustached man in the magic show, elbows me in the ribs periodically to make fun of some dumb thing in the movie. Despite her telling me the jokes, Ollie on her other side hears and laughs at every single one. They also debate a time or two back and forth about the name of an actress in the movie. During one of their debates, Hendry and I steal a secret kiss that is pleasantly time-consuming and has nothing at all to do with superheroes or pizza, except perhaps for the taste.

"Keep in touch, alright?" Hendry tells me, for the first time lowering his mask of joy he's been wearing all day. "Don't be a stranger."

"I don't want to be a stranger. In fact, quite the opposite. I want to be around you. I don't want this to end."

"We'll visit each other," Hendry suggests. "We're only a few hours away. You, at college in Austin ... Me, just north of Houston ..."

I take a breath and brace myself. If I don't tell him the decision I made—one that involved a secret chat with Ollie and Trish— I'm going to burst apart.

"I'm not going back."

Hendry's face flickers in surprise. I might as well have just punched him. "What?"

"I want to transfer to Houston."

His face is blank and disbelieving. I can tell he wants it to be true, but even a bright and strong person like Hendry can fall victim to skepticism from time to time.

"I used the ... *crawling* ship internet ... to do a little research. I took what you said the other night to heart. Ollie has room in his house, so I'm moving in. And ... I want to help *you* go back to college, Hendry. So ..."

"No," he breathes. "No, no. Scott. You—"

"Ollie will have space for the *both* of us." Before Hendry can protest further, I go on. "Forgive me if this is really forward of me to say, but surely your big brother would want you to take every opportunity in life. Your mom wants you to be happy, too. You're so smart and you *deserve* to be in school, and I want to help you do that. Ollie does too. I *need* you to be there with me. Please."

"What ... What about *your* studies? Your plan? Y-You had a plan," he says, stammering and racing to make sense of my unanticipated curveball.

"There's a good program in Houston I can get into. Ollie's house is enormous and really close to campus. I'm talking walking distance, dude. You won't have to pay rent. You can get a job in Houston and send money to your mom and brother, if you want. Doesn't it make sense to fill my life with people who make me a better person? Ollie. You." I smirk, then add, "I'll let Trish continue to grow on me." I smile. "You taught me to go with the flow. Now it's your turn. Please let Ollie and I do this for you. For me. For both of us."

Hendry looks away, light in his eyes. He's working it through in his head. He reconciles with himself, putting the pieces together. His face seems to say: *Is this really happening?*

The look is all I need to feel the deep and penetrating sense of affirmation that my insane, ridiculous choice to fly out of my cage and take a *different* sort of control of my life might be the first right thing I've done in a very long while.

Other than ignore that warning sign on the lido deck, of course.

"It may not work," I confess a while later after poor head-spinning Hendry has had time to process. "We've been sharing a room for just two days. I don't know how we'll be after living together for two semesters. Or more. But I'm willing to take the risk if you are."

Hendry laughs. "You're one of the coolest, most interesting people I've ever met, Scott. I can't believe Ollie would do that for me, too. And ... wow. After spending a day thinking it'd be our last, it suddenly feels an awful lot like our first of many."

I admire the glint of excitement in his eye. I hope that glint turns into fire and sweat tonight when we hit a certain bed on the seventh deck.

"We'll be coming into the registration and enrollment process a tad late, I hope you realize," points out Hendry, worrying on it. "A lot of classes are gonna be filled up."

The control-freak planner deep within me screams and screams from a cage where I've locked him up down inside. "I can swing with that if you can."

"And you're sure they're okay with this?"

"Don't know how you did it," I say, "but Trish is basically in love with you. Took me over four years to get on the frigid princess's 'okay' side, and even still I'll be minding my words to keep the house from burning down. I guess you just have that kind of ... magic."

"Y'know. I think you're right. My mom will want this for me. So will Josiah. I'm kinda scared ... but excited about all this," Hendry confesses, blessing me with the cute pinch of his nose as he thinks on all the possibilities. In truth, I'm pretty damn excited myself. "Yeah!" he says, inspired. "Why the hell not? Let's fucking do it."

"Do what?" asks Trish, who's pulled away from a private back-and-forth with Ollie to pay us some mind.

"Dude-bro stuff," I call back.

She gives us both a look and comes to the wrong conclusion. "I don't care how cute the pair of you are, you can keep your bedroom business to yourselves. Damn, have a little modesty." She sets her mouth into a smirk and turns her attention back to the movie.

Hours later when the flick has finished and my friends say goodnight and head back to the room for one last slumber on the boat, Hendry and I lazily stay on the deck, letting the blanket of glittery darkness embrace us.

His arms wrap around me. His fingers playing along my back and neck. My arms wrap around him, holding his body to mine. We'll have to let go, at least for a little while. Then, I can't wait for whatever's next.

In the whirring silence of the emptied deck, Hendry whispers: "Thanks for taking the journey with me, bromo."

I turn my head, putting my lips right to his ear. "It's only just begun."

In the moonless glow above, the infinite dust of stars Hendry kept bragging about finally reveal themselves in a countless spread of winks and smiles. In them, I see the infinite possibilities. I see the magic and the sandy beach wetted by the waves. I see the ridiculous humor of it all. I see the nerve-seizing fear.

And I'm so fucking ready.

The end.

Printed in Great Britain
by Amazon